THE ILLUSION OF BEING HERE

DAVID HUTTO

PRETENSE PRESS

Published by Pretense Press
Atlanta, Georgia, USA

Copyright 2014

ISBN: 978-0-9905692-0-6 (ebook)
ISBN: 978-0-9905692-1-3 (paperback)

Sometimes when the night was clear,

The moon rode high, the stars seem'd near.

Then came the thought that I'm not here,

Though if I'se not, who'd drink my beer?

Percy of Abbotsford (1737–1789)

What does it take to make you happy—a perfect job or just a beautiful spring morning? What if someone loved you so much that they let you know it every day? Not enough people are receiving love letters.

Paul Gildbridge taught history at the College of Charleston in South Carolina. In his spare time, he wore blue denim shirts, took photographs of the nearby islands and marshes, and read novels by Latin American authors. He was also doing a personal survey of the restaurants in Charleston. Paul Gildbridge should have been happy. Unlike most of us, he was getting love letters by email. But we all want something more. A person who has a diamond wants two diamonds. Even though Paul was in love, he was concerned about his job. Next year, he was going to apply for tenure at his school; this would give him permanent job security. He was worried about getting it, however, and about how being turned down would disrupt his life. If he were granted tenure, there would be diamonds in the night sky, and he would ask Rachel to move down from Virginia to Charleston. She would say yes, they would live in a cottage filled with flowers, and singing mice would dance and clean the cottage. But what if he didn't get tenure? He would be banished like Dante from a city he loved, joining academic refugees on the dusty roads, sleeping in the woods, eating grapes of wrath from a can, and looking for tenure-track jobs. He would also be unable to ask his beloved Rachel to come and live with him. How could he possibly ask her if he didn't even know where he would be living? Paul's department head had told him that he needed better publications to help get tenure, and Paul was working on a book, his first. But would it be published? Would it be good enough?

Sometimes Paul sat in his office, looking out the window past the rows of tin soldiers he had set up along the window sill, thinking about the feel of Rachel's kisses or about the way the sun spilled across the campus and whether it was good light for taking photographs. His mother had given him a camera as a boy, not long after his father abandoned them and disappeared, and Paul had been taking photographs of the place he lived ever since. Other times, when he sat looking out his office window, he contemplated Catherine the Great, the subject of his book, and then his thoughts wandered to St. Petersburg, Russia, where the honey-gold light often bathed the city in amber. That was where he had seen the large statue of Catherine on Nevsky Prospect.

When he was not teaching classes, writing, or

photographing the islands, Paul sometimes visited his Aunt Lindy. Charleston was Paul's hometown, but of his family, only two elderly aunts still lived there. Aunt Lindy had once been a bit of a grande dame during days of crystal glasses with old port wine and visiting authors who wrote elegant stories about quietly broken characters. For the last year, however, Aunt Lindy's mind had increasingly been set free from the dull laws of reality, until one summer day at nine-thirty in the morning. That morning, she died too young, at sixty-seven, and drifted away to be with whoever she imagined God to be. When Paul found out, he called his sister Anna, who was sorry to hear about their aunt's death and even sorrier that her difficult job would keep her from attending the funeral. Paul then called his younger sister, Jan, and then finally their only cousin, Luke Pharo, who lived in Washington, DC.

When they had all been children, Luke's family would come for visits, and all the cousins—Luke, Paul, Anna, and sometimes little Jan—would climb out the bedroom windows at night to make Important Secret Plans in the yard. On warm afternoons, they would catch June bugs, tie threads to the insects' legs, and then hold the threads and watch them fly in helpless buzzing circles. At that age, Paul had kept a collection of dried insects—not on pins in a box but glued to a piece of cardboard that hung from a nail on his bedroom wall. When Luke was visiting, he would sometimes help Paul catch insects for the bedroom display. On rainy afternoons, when they couldn't play outside, the four cousins would talk about irritated ghosts who came back looking for their lost heads, stumbling through the world with their hands outstretched. When they got older and Paul joined the science club at his high school, thought about joining the Navy, or drove his sister Anna to Columbia to see Stevie Nicks, Luke lived somewhere far away with his parents, and in their adult lives, Luke went off into the world. He had moved to Washington after the terrible events in Russia, and even though it had been two years, people in the family still felt sorry for him. Because of Aunt Lindy's funeral, people were coming together, and Luke had come down from Washington. He was now sitting in Paul's apartment, wearing a button-up dark blue shirt.

"I'm going to shower," Paul said, "I'll be out in a few minutes. If you like Scotch—"

Luke looked up with an expression of interest. "Scotch? Hell yeah, I'd like some Scotch. How old is it?"

"Twelve years."

"So you've turned into a civilized man."

"An illusion, of course, but one I like to maintain. I keep my liquid treasure in that treasure cabinet by the door. Just leave some for me so I don't have to kill you."

Paul went into the bathroom and shut the door.

He adjusted the water for the shower, thinking about how it felt to have Luke there, both of them adults now. They remembered each other as children playing on the beach, picking up shells, and throwing icky tendrils of seaweed at each other. As adults, they knew one another very little, but just in the few hours since he had hugged Luke at the airport, Paul felt completely comfortable with him. In some ways, they were very different people, but Luke still seemed like the same person who had taught his cousins to say "Get away from me!" in Japanese. For a few months after he learned it, Paul had used the phrase on other kids at school until it lost its exotic novelty for him.

When Paul came out of the shower, Luke was sitting on the couch, holding a glass of golden Scotch, looking at a calendar that he had taken down from the wall. The picture for that month showed a barefoot woman in a gray dress, standing next to a smoking cauldron over a fire.

"So you got a witch calendar," Luke said.

"Yeah." Paul picked up the Scotch bottle. "I guess I like strong women." Saying this made him think of Rachel.

"Of course these are stereotypes," Luke said. "Real witches look more normal."

"You think?" Paul asked, pouring himself a glass.

Luke nodded. "Yes." He turned a page on the calendar and said, "Tomorrow is Bastille Day. Selia and I were in Paris once on Bastille Day." Selia was

Luke's wife. "Feels like yesterday and a hundred years ago. Kind of strange for a man who's only thirty-four." Paul nodded but said nothing. He was four years older than Luke, so time possibly went even faster for him.

The two cousins went out onto the tiny balcony to sit in the heavy Charleston air. Below the balcony was a small courtyard with a table and two chairs, and next to the table, hibiscus bushes were blooming, their intense orange flowers forcing you to look even if you didn't intend to. Every morning, an old couple wearing straw hats sat drinking coffee at that table down below. That morning, Paul had heard them talking about someone flying across India in a balloon. In a neighboring yard nearby, a palm tree grew up higher than the balcony where Paul and Luke were sitting.

The balcony was small, but in addition to their chairs, Paul had managed to get a tiny table onto it. An African violet sat in a green glazed pot on the small table. A ring of dead leaves drooped around the sides of the pot, and the living leaves in the middle had a yellowish tint.

"You're killing this plant," Luke said.

"God's killing it. I'm just not stopping him. But I should water it." Paul looked at his violet and felt slightly guilty but didn't move to correct his sin.

As they sat quietly sipping Scotch, looking down at the courtyard below, Paul rested his glass on his belly, which didn't see enough exercise. "I'm glad to have you here," he said to Luke.

Luke raised his own glass to drink. "Yeah, me too. We haven't seen each other much since we were kids."

Looking west from the window of the plane, Luke hadn't even tried to avoid the memory of flying toward the low mountains of Appalachia to the west. Yet such remembering was so awful it became a black hole that could suck up all thoughts that came close. As the plane passed over Virginia, he forced his attention to the present, to what he was doing, flying to Charleston after his cousin Paul had called. He wondered how it was going to feel in Charleston, returning to a place that he mostly associated with being a child, coming back now for his aunt's funeral. It had been years since he and Selia had visited Charleston. Most particularly, he hadn't returned to Charleston after he left Moscow, since the city with golden domes had gone dim in his eyes.

Luke had visited and lived many places, and in an irony that echoed with the silent laughter of God, one of the places he had felt the most connection with was Russia. He had learned the history, learned the language, and learned to love the writers. One who he liked especially was Anna Akhmatova, who he read over the years, enough to remember lines from several of her poems: "Rising up from the past, my shadow comes silently to meet me." His own shadow rose up to meet him in San Francisco in April 1969. His father was stationed there with the army, so his mother brought him into the world in a foggy city. As a child he had had nightmares, and the earliest, a dream that repeated, was an old woman coming into a room where he was sitting. Always in the dream she would turn and start walking toward him, but suddenly her head would fall off and roll toward him, saying, "Hello, Luke, hello, Luke". Every time, he woke crying out from that dream. Eventually, the old woman kept her head and went away. Maybe she realized that soon he'd be old enough to understand what was going on in the real world, which is so much more terrifying.

"Yall were always traveling off around the world somewhere. You didn't come back here very often."

"I liked it when we came, though. Will Anna and Jan be here?"

"Jan is driving over, but Anna can't get down from New Jersey. I'm sorry I won't get to see Ian and Lucy." These were Anna's children, who Paul would get on the floor to play with, snorting and making animal noises, sometimes an elephant, sometimes a bear.

"Maybe she can't come because of the kids," Luke said. "How is she doing?"

"She's doing OK. Not long ago she started a new job in Philadelphia, and she really likes it. She does publicity for an arts group."

"I'm sorry I won't see her."

"Yeah, me too," Paul said. "I wanted to take the

kids to the bookstore and let them pick something out." Paul thought about how Ian had played with the toy soldiers in his office, putting them up into groups of three, and then the middle soldier in each group fell over and died. When Paul asked why only the middle ones were dying, Ian had said, "The bad guys are in the middle".

"And how is Jan?" Luke asked about Paul's youngest sister.

"You remember Richard? The loud guy?"

"Was he loud?" Luke asked. He stuck a finger in his left ear to scratch it.

"Yeah, he couldn't talk without making you want to back up. Anyway, they broke up. Now she's with a guy she really likes, who works for CNN. She doesn't love her job, though. Getting tired of teaching those monsters in junior high."

"Is she coming over?"

"In the morning. She should get here in time."

"I'm glad I'll see her," Luke said. "Do you expect a lot of people at the funeral?"

"Yeah, I'm not sure." Paul tried to picture who might show up. "Aunt Lindy wasn't all that old, but a lot of her friends have died. Even so, she's a Gildbridge, so that should draw some people. People notice that name here. I've run into that all my life." He took a long drink of Scotch, held it gratefully a moment in his mouth, then swallowed. "And technically, I'm not even a Gildbridge."

"What do you mean?" Luke asked. "All the sisters were Gildbridges. That makes you one." Luke referred to his and Paul's mothers, along with their Aunt Lindy and Aunt Maryanne.

"But it's the custom in this country to take the father's last name, right? The way you did. But after my father ran away, I started using Mama's last name." The disappearance of his father had always been an embarrassment to Paul, and he blamed his father for their financial struggles after that.

"So what? You're still a Gildbridge. You're part of that family."

"Alright, yeah. In that sense, you're one too. This family has been in Charleston a long time. 'The family of fools is very old.' You know that saying? So you know—" He turned to Luke. "I know you've been all over the world."

"Foreign Service moves you around," Luke said.

"Sounds like it. But I know I've gotten mixed up where yall lived."

"It's not that hard to remember. We were in Moscow for two years, Berlin before that, Beijing before that. But we did travel, so maybe it was confusing."

Paul hesitated, wondering whether to mention what happened in Moscow. Instead he said, "I thought yall were in Czechoslovakia."

"No, we just visited there."

"Then why did I think that? I was sure yall lived in Prague."

"Nope."

"Oh man." Paul pushed up from his chair and asked, "You hungry? I think it's time to be hungry."

"Yes!" Luke exclaimed. "Yes I am. I'm starving."

"Well then. We're in the right town if you like to eat. And who doesn't like to eat?" He laughed and patted his belly. "You can see I do. You like seafood?"

"Yeah, I like seafood. But not raw oysters."

"That's a sad prejudice, cousin. You need to work on that. But fortunately, we cook some of the food."

They left the house and headed for a small restaurant several blocks away. The evening was sultry, as a Charleston summer evening will probably be. "Sultry" of course is poetic language meaning too hot and too much humidity, but how could tourists be induced to come to Charleston in the summer without poetry? There were still a couple of hours of daylight, and tourists were out on the streets, an occasional carriage went by, the horse clopping along slowly as if it was bored. Or it may have been a perfectly contented horse with a bored expression. As they walked along, Paul pointed out features of the city that he liked, pastel colored houses, pots of flowers in window sills, or fancy ironwork. "I love Charleston," he said. "I can't imagine living anywhere else."

"Does it make you think of Saint Petersburg?" Luke asked.

"Florida?"

"No, St. Petersburg, Russia."

"Well…no."

At the restaurant a waitress with very long black hair brought two cold glasses of dark beer, and Paul asked Luke, "So why did you say Charleston reminds you of St. Petersburg? I don't see that." He thought about the three trips he had made to the city, twice with Luke and Selia.

Luke took a long drink of the cold beer and sighed with satisfaction. "I wouldn't exactly say it *reminds* me of St. Petersburg, but…there's something that, um, it makes me think of St. Petersburg."

"Like what?" Without realizing it, Paul was tapping a finger in time to the music playing in the restaurant.

"Partly they're both port cities with rivers. Maybe that's part of it. I think it's mostly all the Greek influence. When I walk around here or when I walk around in St. Petersburg, I keep seeing Greek architecture."

"Sure," Paul said. "But that's true in a lot of places. What I mostly remember of St. Petersburg is the palaces, and you're right, they have a Greekiness. But the place seemed so Russian to me, like that church covered in onion domes." He recalled walking along the canal with Luke and Selia, looking at the indescribable domed church ahead of them. When they went inside, Selia began telling him about some of the icons.

"The Church of the Spilt Blood," Luke said.

"Yeah, that's it. Church of the Spilt Blood. That

name carries a certain poetry, doesn't it?" Paul half smiled to think of it, not even really a smile. "That's a delightful name."

"It's because of blowing up the tsar there they gave it that name."

"It's lovely. So maybe it's because I know Charleston so well, but they seem pretty different to me. Anyhow—" He picked up his menu. "I guess we should choose what to eat. I recommend the she-crab soup."

"As in female crab?"

"As female as they get. Highly recommended."

"OK, I'll try the soup, but maybe, this uh—" Luke looked through the menu. "Some shrimp." He closed his menu. "Yeah, it's a shame Anna can't come."

"Yep, it is." Paul shrugged. "Once you get other people in your life it gets complicated."

Luke closed his eyes for a second, looked around the room, then turned back to his cousin. "What about you," he asked. "You got anybody in your life?"

"I sure do." Paul smiled. He thought of Rachel standing with her arms held wide, looking at him and pretending to sing along with a song by Suzanne Vega on the radio.

"Will I meet her?"

"Not this time, I'm afraid. She lives in Richmond, Virginia."

"Not so far from where I live. What does she do?"

"She's a potter. She has a studio behind her house."

"A potter. She make a living as a potter?"

"Yeah, she goes to a lot of shows, and she does make a living. Her name's Rachel. I work with her sister at the college, and I met Rachel when she came down for the Spoleto festival. But she lives in Richmond."

"Richmond's a good ways from here," Luke said. "How's the long-distance thing working out?" He lifted his fingers away from his cheek and gestured with them.

"Yeah…" Paul frowned. "It's frustrating. I think we're ready to be together, but she's there and I'm here. Yeah, I don't like this distance." He shook his head a bit, a faint grimace crossing his lips. He thought of how often he sat in his apartment, wanting to comment on things to Rachel, but she wasn't there. Even if they were useless comments—"looks cloudy today"—he wanted to share them with her.

"So could she move? I mean, basically she's working out of her house, right?"

"Yeah, her studio is there. I want to ask her to move down here, but I want to be more secure in my job. Security matters. I learned that growing up, since we didn't have enough of it."

Luke raised his eyebrows. "Are you insecure in your job? Do college professors get fired?"

Paul shrugged and shook his head at the same time. "Yes they do, if they don't get tenure. They are told to get the hell out."

"And you're thinking—"

"No, I'm not really thinking anything. But I don't have it yet, and I don't know what's gonna happen." He remembered the biologist who didn't get tenure last year, remembered the conversation with his own department head about publishing more.

"Then I'll wish you luck." Luke raised his glass and drank.

"If it involves drinking beer, I'll wish me luck, too," Paul said, and also drank. He set the glass down, saw an acquaintance and waved, then turned back to Luke. "You reminded me of when I came to see yall in Russia. I'm envious of how good you are in speaking Russian. I know I should know it, but…"

"I've had a lot of practice by now, you know."

Paul had taken two years of Russian in college, after he had decided to focus on Russian history. "I could practice till the cows turn blue," he said. "The best I'd come out with would sound something like 'me need toilet for self'. The main thing I learned about Russian is how freakishly hard it is." As the full terrifying panoply of Russian grammar was gradually revealed, Paul had begun to realize how inconceivable it was to learn such a language. "I know it's a problem that I can't read it very well, but I get through some things with a dictionary." He paused and glanced around the room, wondering whether a student who he knew was still working there, then he looked back at Luke. "You know, sometimes I envy what you've done with the

Foreign Service," he said. "I think it would be pretty interesting to live places like you've lived."

"Sometimes it is," Luke replied. "But you know…" He sighed slightly. "After a while, I just started to think I was living life like other people, get up, go to work, come home, eat dinner, get up, go to work. To tell you the truth, right now I'm thinking what the hell's the point."

Paul thought about Rachel, or reading a novel by Isabel Allende, or eating a plate of oysters. "Maybe the point is just to get to the good things. I guess. Isn't the real point the things we enjoy?"

"But are good things now and then enough?" Luke asked. "The reason we're alive is to experience pleasure? Dogs do that."

"OK, it seems oversimplified when you put it like that."

"Yeah," Luke said, "it seems kind of meaningless."

"Oh no." Paul waved his hands in front of him. "I'm not saying meaningless. I don't think what we do is meaningless. That would be too cynical."

"I'm not cynical either," Luke said." I'm perplexed." They were silent for a minute, then he asked, "So do you like your job?"

"Yeah, I like my job. There's things I don't like, of course, but I like it. I'm trying to keep it. I said I don't have tenure yet, but I'm writing a book that I hope will make sure I get it. It's a book about Catherine the Great."

"Oh yeah?" Luke sat a little straighter. "Seriously? Why didn't you tell me this?"

"Well, I would have. I've just now gotten to it. You've only been here—" Paul looked at his watch. "Five hours."

"OK, so what's the book?"

"I think the idea for this book might have started the first time I came to see yall in Russia. When we went up to St. Petersburg and saw places associated with Catherine."

"Huh!" Luke's eyes were fixed hard on Paul.

Paul leaned slightly forward and said, "But there's something way more interesting to tell you. You ever hear of Henry Middleton?"

Luke thought a few seconds, then said, "I don't think so."

"Middleton is a big name here in South Carolina, and the Gildbridges are related to him. He's one of our ancestors. Rich guy, money just fell off him, and you can still go visit his house out at Middleton Place. Or what's left of it. So when I told Aunt Maryanne that I was working on a book about Catherine the Great, she told me that Henry Middleton wrote to Catherine the Great and got a reply."

"That is very interesting."

"No no," Paul said. "We're not there yet. And then she told me that the letter came down in the family, that we still have it."

"Seriously?" Luke stared astonished at Paul.

"Aunt Maryanne told me this about six months ago. She said Aunt Lindy had the letter."

"From Catherine the Great? Did she look at it? Aunt Maryanne?"

"No, she just knew Aunt Lindy had it."

"How did she know it was from Catherine the Great? Did you see it? Is it from Catherine?"

Paul grimaced. "Now we get to the screwed up part. I can't find it. Aunt Maryanne said the story in the family has always been that the letter is from Catherine."

"And what did Aunt Lindy say? She had the letter, right?"

"For at least a year now you couldn't hold a conversation with Aunt Lindy."

The waitress came up to set two bowls of soup on the table. "Two more beers?" she asked.

"Yes," Paul replied. The waitress walked away and he continued. "So I asked Aunt Lindy about the letter anyway, but when I asked her about it, she just said, 'You're a good boy, you're gonna write me a letter.' She was sort of crazy and not crazy at the same time. After she said, 'You're gonna write me a letter' the next time I went to see her she said, 'Where's my letter?' It was pretty strange."

He stopped and took a spoonful of soup. "This is good," he said.

"And Aunt Maryanne doesn't know anything about where it might be?" Luke asked. He also took a spoonful of soup, and added, "This is really good. Why do they call it she-crab?"

"I don't know why they call it that. And no, Aunt Maryanne didn't have a clue." Paul shook his head slightly and tightened his lips. "I'd love to have that letter, too. If I had a letter from Catherine that nobody had ever seen? Man. Man oh man."

Luke puffed his cheeks a bit and blew air out. "Oh yeah. You could publish just on the letter."

"I'm hoping it might turn up still," Paul said. "But it'll just be a lucky chance, I guess, if it does."

"You looked in the attic?" Luke asked. "I remember a lot of stuff up there."

"Oh yeah, it's full of stuff. It looks like it did from when we were kids. You couldn't find your own name up there."

"I remember a bunch of old clothes hanging along one side."

"They're still there." Paul also remembered that Luke had been afraid of that attic. What he didn't remember was that when he was even younger, he had been afraid, too.

"Are they? Jan and Anna used to dress up and have tea parties up there in the attic. I didn't like it much."

As a good Gildbridge, Aunt Lindy had attended St. Michael's Episcopal Church. For many years, good Charleston citizens had been walking to the church in the summer, dressed uncomfortably in ties and jackets, walking and breathing slowly in that heavy coastal air. In Charleston, the worship of God requires discomfort, which probably seems unfair, but no doubt God is making note of all that damp devotion. Paul only lived a few blocks from the church, which he also attended a couple of times a month, so on Saturday afternoon he and Luke walked down Meeting Street toward the church. As they walked, sweat was beaded up on their foreheads and rolled down their temples.

"We're not gonna live through the service," Luke said.

"You sort of get used to the heat if you live here," Paul said.

"Yeah, sure. People in Hell are saying, 'You know, after the first million years—.'"

The tall bell tower of the church was visible from blocks away, an intentional symbol of God's power, which He had wisely entrusted to His faithful servants at St. Michael's. The front of the church had four large columns and a shaded porch area, with a palm tree growing to one side. Standing on the porch, out of the sun, was a group of friends and relatives who came for the funeral. A woman with straight brown hair, wearing a navy blue dress and a black hat, stood near a column. She was fairly large and solidly built, like her older brother Paul. "Luke!" she cried when she saw him and came over to hug him. Jan had bright eyes, deep blue, pale eyebrows to match her pale complexion, and a wide happy smile.

"Hello, Jan," Luke said and put his arms around

her. He hugged her tightly and held on for a moment, then kissed her on the cheek and stepped back. "It's good to see you," he said.

"It's been three years, hasn't it?" she replied.

"How long are you staying?" he asked.

"Till tomorrow."

"Is that Luke?" a voice behind Jan asked. Jan turned around, and she and Luke stepped into the shade under the porch. Aunt Maryanne stood there, dressed in an expensive dark gray dress, with a light straw hat. Unlike Jan or Paul, she was thin, with narrow facial features, a small nose and mouth and slightly sunken cheeks. The skin of her face and neck was now loose and wrinkled, but from her eyes it was clear that a sharp mind was looking through them. "So our periodic prodigal returns," she said. "I guess to get you to come to Charleston next time I'll have to die."

"Hello, Aunt Maryanne," Luke said. He gave her a hug, ducking a bit from her wide hat.

"And I'm not getting any younger, you know," she said, hugging him. "I'm up to sixty-eight already."

"That's not that old," Luke said.

"You let me know when you get to be my age." She stepped back, adjusted her hat, which had been knocked to the side, and said, "The years go fast but the days go slow. So how are you doing, Luke?"

"I just came down from Washington yesterday," he said.

"Yes, I know you did. But my question is how

you're doing. Oh, I think they're calling us to come in for the service. I'll have to ask you again later." She took his arm, and walking slowly, they went through the door of the church. She directed Luke to lead her down to the front, with Paul and Jan behind them. Near the front of the church they opened the door into a box pew and all sat down. In front was the coffin of Aunt Lindy, closed and surrounded by large flower arrangements, lilies of sorrow, roses of remembrance, even carnations of fondness. Paul wondered if Luke had ever been in this church, but didn't think so, although he remembered that Luke was raised Episcopalian. Paul loved the church, with the white walls, a wooden balcony up above, and the stained glass windows along the sides. He had seen two friends get married here, had been to his mother's funeral here. If he were to get married, would it be here? He hoped so, but it was very strange to think of standing down front with Rachel in the spot where Lindy's coffin now stood.

After the funeral the family and many of the friends gathered at Aunt Maryanne's house on Legare Street, down near the Battery, the point of land where both rivers came together and the bay began. The table in the dining room was covered with corn pudding, crab cakes, bean salad, barbecued chicken fingers, more food than anyone could eat, though they tried, and on a smaller table nearby were a dozen photographs of Aunt Lindy in frames, with yellow roses lying in front of the photographs. Belinda Gildbridge had been plain looking when she was young in the old black and white photographs, but as an old woman there was a certain grace about her in the colored photographs, as she dressed well and always seemed to have an expression of self-confidence.

By early evening most of the guests had left, and several people were sitting in wicker chairs on the porch, which was built, like so many in Charleston, to face the bay and catch breezes coming up from that direction. Terracotta pots of red geraniums sat around the edges of the porch, and a white table had been placed in the middle with a pitcher and glasses. Paul, Luke, and Jan sat on white wicker chairs, each holding a glass of lemonade. Paul felt very glad to have Jan and Luke sitting there. It was sad that they were together because of Aunt Lindy's death, but it was good to be with his sister and his cousin. With them sat Aunt Maryanne, the last of the four sisters. Lucille, Paul's mother, had died first, only forty-nine, then Fanny, Luke's mother, died the following year at forty-eight. Now Belinda was gone, leaving only Maryanne.

"Whatever wisdom we have in this family, I guess it's up to me to keep it now," Aunt Maryanne said.

"We're old enough to help you keep it," Paul said.

"I'm not feeling reassured," she replied, fanning herself with her straw hat. "It wasn't that much to keep anyway. When we were all girls, I think I was twenty-one, so Fanny would have been thirteen, Frank Sinatra came to town. We couldn't get tickets to hear him, but we decided we'd go down to the theater, and when he came out the back we'd ask for his autograph. So four stupid girls go get in that old Ford we had then and drive downtown, without telling Mama. When we got to the theater, we were surprised to see that other people had the same brilliant idea, so there was a crowd. Lucille brought a bag of cookies she had made, because she thought Frank Sinatra would like some cookies. There we all stood, until it started to rain, until we all looked like a crowd of drowned rats waiting for autographs. We never saw Frank Sinatra, but we did see Mama when we got home. We were chilled from the rain, but Mama gave us a warm discussion."

Sitting with them on the porch were another woman who Paul vaguely knew from years back and a man named Peter Gogol, an old friend of Aunt Lindy. He was tall and thin, as if he were made entirely of angles. His head was half bald from the front, with thin straight hair hanging down in the back. He also had a prominent Adam's apple and large teeth. Aunt Lindy had always called Peter Gogol by his full name. "Maybe I just like the name," she would say. She definitely had her eccentricities, which gave people real opinions about her.

"Do yall remember that poodle Aunt Lindy had that used to steal sea grass baskets?" Jan asked.

"Belinda never had a poodle," Aunt Maryanne said.

"Are you sure? I thought she had a poodle."

"No, she used to always have Pomeranians when she was still keeping dogs."

"OK, I guess it must have been a Pomeranian then. But it used to steal baskets."

"How could a dog steal baskets?" Luke asked.

"Well, I'm telling you," Jan said. "Aunt Lindy had one of those sea grass baskets down on a bottom shelf of a bookcase. Isn't that right, Aunt Maryanne?"

"That's the story I know."

"So she had this basket down there, one of those kind of flat ones, and one day she found it was missing. I don't know why she wanted it down there, but it was gone. She looked all over for it and never could find it, so she figured one of the people that she hired to do things around the house must have taken it. So she bought another one. And it disappeared. So she bought another one."

"Yeah," Paul added, "and she said the people who made the baskets must be breaking in and stealing them."

Luke pursed his lips and looked doubtful. "And she never found any of those baskets? Does a dog eat baskets?"

"Hold on," Jan said. "I've got to tell the whole thing. I think Aunt Lindy bought her fourth basket, and finally she saw the dog with the basket in its mouth, running off around the corner. It was stuffing all those baskets behind the couch."

Peter Gogol threw his head back and laughed. "Hahaha, I never heard that! Lindy was such a character."

Paul laughed as well and said, "Seems like the dog was a character."

"And why was the dog doing that?" Luke asked.

"You know…" Jan leaned forward and lowered her voice. "No matter how much they tortured it, it never would say."

"They didn't torture it enough," Paul said.

Peter Gogol laughed again. "Lindy had some strange things happen to her," he said. "You know about her house keeper," he said.

"Oh yeah," Paul replied. "That was weird."

"I felt sorry for Belinda," Aunt Maryanne said.

"What about the housekeeper?" Luke asked. Paul realized that Luke must feel like he was in on a conversation where everyone else actually knew all the details already. It showed how much Luke had gotten beyond contact with the family.

"It was about two years ago," Peter Gogol said, turning toward Luke. "Lindy was in a wheelchair then, couldn't walk at all. Oh, well, I guess most people in a wheelchair can't. So she hired a woman to keep house for her, Coralue Jordan. Coralue was in her sixties, not all that old, but she wasn't healthy, only nobody knew that. Maybe Coralue didn't know it, either. This happened one evening when Coralue and Lindy were sitting in the living room watching TV. Lindy didn't like to sit in the wheelchair all the time, and I wouldn't either if it was me. So she had Coralue move her into one of those big stuffed chairs that are more comfortable, and then Coralue sat down in another one. I think they were watching Wheel of Fortune, something like that, anyway Lindy decided she wanted to go to bed. So she called Coralue, but Coralue didn't answer. Lindy said she called her several times, then kind of yelled at her, and finally threw a book at her. I believe she said it was a gardening book. The book hit Coralue and her head just kind of tilted over to one side, like a dead person's head will do. That was when Lindy picked up the phone on the table next to her, called an ambulance and said, 'I think my housekeeper is dead.' They must have been pretty confused about that. Or maybe they deal with a lot of that kind of thing."

"That is a weird story," Luke said.

"And after that Lindy never wanted another old woman working for her. She said one dropping dead was enough, and after that she only hired these young girls that you used to see over there all the time. It was hard for her to keep help, though. She could be pretty sharp with those young girls, who don't know when an old person is just sort of cranky, you know. Lindy could be a real inspector general when something didn't suit her."

"Well she had her good points, too, now," Aunt Maryanne said.

"Oh, I'm not criticizing Lindy," Peter Gogol said. "I loved her. I'm certainly going to miss her."

They sat on the porch telling stories about Lindy, and as they sat talking, some of the mourners held drinks, some moved back and forth in rocking chairs. At one time Lindy had walked the earth herself, had sat in those very chairs, had told stories, and now it was all in the past. Did that past still exist in another part of the universe, the place where the earth had been when it occurred? Maybe all that remained was memories and objects. Inside Lindy's house on a shelf stood a porcelain doll dressed as a Norwegian girl, and people might say that doll was evidence of the past, that Lindy had bought it and put it there. But if no one remembered that she had done that, the doll would still be there in the present. So what did that doll say about the past? No doubt objects tell us something about what happened. *What* they say, however, isn't clear, as they often seem to speak in a language we can't understand. What would it take to make sure Aunt Lindy truly was not forgotten? Perhaps everyone sitting on the porch should have put their drinks down, gotten up from their rocking chairs, and gone out to start measuring the ground, getting ready to build a pyramid. As a historian, Paul should have known this.

"Lindy was a feisty woman," Peter Gogol said.

"And she was like that when she was shopping," Aunt Maryanne said. "Belinda just loved to shop. You know she loved nice things. When we were in Egypt, she saw some scarves she wanted at a street stall, and I bet she spent half an hour standing there negotiating over those scarves, and both her and that Egyptian man didn't know one word the other one was speaking. But my land, they both had a good time. You should've seen Belinda. She'd start to walk away, and that man would wave his arms, and I guess he was saying, 'Wait wait' and she'd turn back around. I looked at five other stalls while she was buying three scarves."

"She did have a lot of beautiful things," Paul said. "You can just walk through her house and see things from all over the world."

"And those dolls everywhere," Jan said. "She sure loved dolls. And she had the nicest jewelry, with that gorgeous amber necklace."

"She only wore that when she was wearing black," Aunt Maryanne said.

The Witch in Moscow: "Give your wife my blessings"

The Russian word for "witch" is "vyedma". If you're looking for a witch in Russia, that's what to ask for. The word comes from an old-fashioned word "vyedat", which means "to know". The original idea was probably that a vyedma was a woman who knows things. Maybe she can know who you're going to marry, or what color your baby's eyes will be, or the words to a song that's not even written yet that they'll sing at your funeral. But what if the witch can see things that are clear to her but not to you?

WHEN LUKE LIVED in Russia, he met a *vyedma* in Moscow, a dark gypsy woman with one green eye and one blue eye, as if there was a kaleidoscope looking out. The meeting happened in July, on one of those hot sticky days filled with tourists who are all over downtown Moscow in the summer. If you're looking for a tourist instead of a witch, other than Red Square, the place to look is Old Arbat Street, which runs at an angle into New Arbat Street. New Arbat is simply another modern boulevard where the city feels big and busy and proud of being modern. The smaller Old Arbat has been closed off into a pedestrian street, lined with restaurants and cafes, with shops selling tourist merchandise. Japanese and American and French tourists go into the stores to buy amber jewelry or embroidered cloths, or they browse the stands in the middle of the street selling cheap trash like T shirts with the profile of Vladimir Lenin against McDonalds' golden arches.

Luke was on his way that day in July to meet a friend who was in Moscow for a few days. It was a friend Luke was not especially close to by then, someone he had known back in college and gone to see the Rolling Stones with. What they now had in common was only the memories of the old days, but the memories were still strong, and they agreed to meet on Arbat for a beer. From the metro stop to get there Luke walked through the underpass beneath the busy boulevard nearby. During the summer that underpass is filled with crowds of people, from visitors passing through to small-time merchants who can carry all their merchandise and set up in a convenient spot. Most of what's sold in the underpass is aimed at people who want souvenirs of Russia: T shirts, wooden spoons and bowls, so many nesting dolls you'd think the round-headed little creatures were breeding, and bootleg CDs of western music. Luke walked on past all of it without a glance, as he had already lived in Moscow for over a year, and whatever interest he had in these things to start with had worn out already. He hurried toward the stairs to go from the underpass when he saw the gypsy woman sitting on the ground. She had large pieces of cardboard spread out beside her, and lying on the cardboard were a couple of dozen icons, in several sizes, from three inches tall to a foot high. They were new, as most icons sold to tourists are, including the ones that have been made to look old. Because of his wife Selia's interest in icons, Luke stopped for a glance. He didn't really expect to find anything of real interest, but he had gotten into the habit of looking. In the very middle of the other icons, leaning up against the wall, was a painting of the angel Gabriel, dressed in a red robe trimmed with gold. Partly over the red robe was a dark gray one, and the angel had dark black wings. Selia had seen this icon in a museum and said that if she ever found a copy of it she wanted to buy it. Since then Luke had looked for it whenever he saw icons for sale, and here suddenly it was.

Luke looked at the gypsy, who sat staring ahead, not paying much attention to him. The woman sat cross legged on the ground. She had black hair and was wearing a dark blue blouse with a striped skirt of various colors. She also wore a necklace of amber beads, practically not beads at all, but large pieces of irregularly shaped amber. Luke noticed the contrast of the amber necklace against the dark blue of the blouse, then he looked again at the icon of Gabriel, happy that he had found it.

"How much for this icon?" he asked the gypsy. "In the middle. Of Gabriel?"

The gypsy turned and looked at it, then turned toward him. "I'm not selling it," she said. "That one is mine."

Luke felt irritated that the woman had put the icon out if she didn't want to sell it, and he was also disappointed that he had found this and now couldn't buy it. "I really want it," he said. "It's for my wife. She's been looking for just this one, and if you'll sell it to me I'll pay a good price." He knew it was foolish to say this, giving the gypsy an opening to charge far too much, but he especially wanted to take this icon home to Selia.

"Then give your wife my blessings," the gypsy said. "But this icon is mine and I can't sell it."

Luke knelt down on the gypsy's level, hoping that he still might talk her into it. He had the idea that it's easier to talk to people in a personal way when you're on the same level. Crowds of people were passing up and down the steps next to them, so he turned slightly to the side to keep from creating an obstacle.

He looked at the gypsy, who now looked him in the eyes, and he saw the color of her eyes, the one green and one blue. "My wife—" he began again, but she interrupted him.

"Your wife," she said, "is not looking for anything, but you are."

"Yes," he said. "I'm looking for an icon. For her."

"No," the gypsy said. "You're looking for something else." She looked hard at him, directly in the eyes, then lifted her hand, with one finger pointing. "My name is Bella," she said, "and I will show you what you're looking for. Look at the icon." She turned and pointed to the icon of Gabriel. Luke had no idea what she was talking about and started to think she was a little crazy, but he looked at the icon. After a couple of seconds, the angel in the picture turned his head to look at Luke. Then the angel's wings began waving back and forth, and he turned, the wings moved faster, and his feet lifted from the ground so that he was flying. He stayed within the frame of the picture, but the ground beneath him was moving, until Luke had a vague sensation of riding on a flying carpet, looking over the edge at a blurred rushing of images. When the picture slowed down, it didn't look painted, but instead looked like a small TV screen, with a lifelike image, and Gabriel flew out of view. Within the frame was a stretch of water with the sun shining on it. Boats with white sails and colored flags flapping in the breeze were coming across the water. In part of the picture nearby, tall grasses were growing by the water.

"What is this?" Luke asked Bella.

"I don't tell things," she said. "I only show them. You are looking for something, and I show it to you."

As amazed as he was by the moving icon, he also felt a little angry at her mysterious response. "But I'm not looking for this," he said. "I don't even know what it is, or where it is."

But the witch remained silent. After a moment he stood up. People were still crowding by, and no one seemed to have noticed anything unusual when the picture was moving.

"Skolko?" he heard someone nearby say with a heavy accent, a tourist asking the price of a doll. *How much*?

Luke looked back down and the icon again had the painted angel Gabriel standing as before. The witch Bella stared ahead and no longer appeared interested in him.

"Did you read this?" Luke asked. "About these people in a balloon?" The cousins sat drinking coffee and reading the newspaper in Paul's apartment, with the air conditioner turned up to keep out the heat that already stalked the streets. Though he lived in a sweltering climate, Paul liked to keep his apartment very cool.

He slowly lowered his paper, shifting his concentration away from what he was reading, and looked up. "What balloon?"

"There's a couple of people from Spain trying to

fly across India in a hot air balloon, from Bombay to Calcutta." Paul always got the *New York Times* on Sunday morning, to see what weird craziness had afflicted the world lately, and to read the editorials that tried to examine the root causes of that weird craziness.

"Well, everybody should have a hobby," he said, and lifted his paper again. "I think the neighbors were talking about that a couple of days ago."

"Along the way they're going to be throwing out pictures of doves, drawn by Picasso."

"If they threw out real doves, they could fly around the balloon," Paul said. "Oh." He lowered his paper suddenly. "You know the reading of the will is in an hour. It's at ten o'clock."

"What?" Luke looked startled and glanced at the clock. "At ten? I better hop in the shower."

Outside the house where Aunt Lindy's lawyer had his office, a house that an architect had lived in while young, before he was successful, was a statue of a dog. The statue was molded from cement and stood on the small porch beside the front door. The dog was painted bright yellow to go with the orange color of the house. "That dog reminds me of statues in China," Luke said.

"Nothing Chinese around here," Aunt Maryanne replied.

"The Peking Rainbow is just two blocks from here," Paul said.

"Well then," she said. "I guess we're in Chinatown."

When they first stepped into the lawyer's office the phone rang, and while he spoke on the phone Paul looked around at the room. There was a diploma on the wall from Emory Law School in Atlanta. The room could have been a living room at one time, where someone may have watched football on TV while rooting for the Green Bay Packers, or opened Christmas presents, pretending to like them because Christmas is a happy time. The room was now decorated with expensive furnishings, upholstered dark red furniture, and large bright photographs of Greek islands in oak frames. Standing on a bookshelf was a pottery jug decorated to look like the ancient Greek pots. The lawyer's head was also a bit like a Greek pot, since he was beginning to go bald, though he was only in his late thirties. He was also clean shaven, with short hair, and his ears drew attention. The ears were normal in size, but turned outward so that they seemed unusually large. He was wearing a dark suit and a deep red tie with a white shirt. The only people gathered now in the orange house with the Chinese dog were Paul, Luke, Aunt Maryanne, and the lawyer.

"So you're all family of Belinda Gildbridge?" the lawyer asked. "I know that you're her sister," he said to Aunt Maryanne.

"And these are her nephews," Aunt Maryanne said.

"Alright. I wasn't sure who would be here, and so that yall didn't have to sit through a lot of lawyer language, I prepared a quick summary of how the will disposes of Belinda Gildbridge's belongings. Of course I'll give you a copy of the will in the original, but I thought it might be easier for now if we worked with the summary."

"I never liked the way lawyers talk anyway," Aunt Maryanne said. "There's enough hot air in Charleston."

"I agree with you there," the lawyer said. "We do pontificate sometimes. I want to begin by advising you that this will was prepared three years ago, prior to the gradual exacerbation of Ms. Gildbridge's illness, when she was still of sound mind. I'm assuming there are no objections to the will, or at least none that I've been informed of."

"I don't think there are any," Aunt Maryanne said.

"Alright, then. Then I'll furnish yall with the basic breakdown. Although the categories aren't comparable in scope or significance, the will is divided into three sections: currency, personal effects, and dwellings. To begin with the currency, Ms. Gildbridge has left $5,000 to her church, St. Michael's Episcopal Church, $5,000 to her nephew, Luke Pharo. That's one of you two gentlemen?"

"That's me," Luke said.

"There's also $5,000 to Jan Watson and $15,000 to Anna Woodleburg. Of course I'll be dispatching letters informing them of the bequest. The next category of the will is longer, disposal of personal effects. That's basically everything Ms. Gildbridge owned. Some things are named and disposed of, but anything that isn't specifically itemized goes to her sister." He looked again at Aunt Maryanne.

"She told me she would do that," Aunt Maryanne said.

"Alright. First is her clothing. She stipulated in the will for you to take anything you want, with all remaining clothing to be given to the Charleston Stage Company, operating out of the Dock Street Theatre."

"That's interesting," Luke said. "So she was a theater fan."

"Well I never knew it," Aunt Maryanne said. "When did she ever go to the theater?"

The lawyer continued. "There is also a bequest of all silver and china to the Gibbs Art Museum, with the amendment that if the museum doesn't want them, then the silver and china should also go to St. Michael's Episcopal Church. Several pieces of jewelry are also named…"

The lawyer continued to name objects and recipients of objects, so many fine things, glass dishes, bright pottery, and beautiful furniture. So many ways the soil of the earth can be fashioned into things that humans like—silica made into glass, clay shaped into pottery, elements of the soil converted into trees and fashioned into tables—the lawyer named these fine things and described where they should be moved to. Thus we work so hard to move the dirt around.

"That's all the personal effects specifically itemized

in the will," the lawyer continued. "The remainder of Ms. Gildbridge's belongings go to you." The lawyer again looked at Aunt Maryanne. "The final category in the will is the disposal of her dwellings. Ms. Gildbridge had two houses, her main residence on East Bay and a smaller beach house out at Foley Beach. The house at Foley Beach is left to Paul Gildbridge."

"Oh my God," Paul said. Aunt Lindy gave him a house? A house?

Luke turned to Paul and said, "Congratulations. You'll be a landowner, like our ancestor Middleton."

"Maybe not quite like Middleton," Aunt Maryanne said.

"Man," Paul said. "I really didn't expect that." He smiled quickly, then frowned faintly, as his expressions showed confusion over suddenly owning a house.

"I always thought you should be a home owner," Aunt Maryanne said. "I told Belinda she should do that. A man can't get married without a house. Now you can give up this foolish bachelor life."

"I wasn't just waiting for a house, Aunt Maryanne."

"Then what have you been waiting on?"

"The house on East Bay has a pending disposition," the lawyer continued. "It's been provisionally left to the Charleston Doll Collectors' Cooperative in order to create a doll museum in Charleston, to be called the Gildbridge Doll Museum."

"Oh, Belinda and her dolls," Aunt Maryanne said. "She was always overboard with those dolls."

"That's the basic provisions of the will," the lawyer said. "So I'll be…oh, there's one more thing. I nearly overlooked this, but I would have caught it later. I'll just read you this part, let's see, it's–'Because my nephew Luke Pharo is so interested in Russia, I leave him the letter from Catherine–'"

"Ah!" Paul cried out.

"'–which is in the middle drawer of the small mahogany desk in the hall.'"

"The letter!" Paul said.

"Oh, don't you remember?" Aunt Maryanne said. "I told you about that."

Luke turned to Paul. "Did you look in that desk?"

"I'm not sure. I looked all over the house, but I might have missed it."

Luke began school in Japan, and for a few years he read Japanese as well as English. From his father's career in the army, the family moved around the world, but wherever they went, his mother would try to immerse them in that culture, so that their household took on a Japanese feeling while they lived in Japan. They ate Japanese food, which Luke loved, and on one occasion his mother exclaimed to someone who had come over, "Luke even likes the fish!" She was so serious about Japanese culture that during the Setsuban festival in February she would toss handfuls of beans around the house, and the family began taking their shoes off in the house, including Luke's father when he came home in his uniform from the army base. When most Americans eat miso soup in a sushi restaurant, they're looking for the experience of a foreign cuisine. As Luke grew older, however, miso soup would take him back to childhood memories, back to snowy winter days, sitting at the kitchen table. In later years he also thought of himself as looking at nature sometimes with Japanese eyes: a line of hills as it ran down to a river, the swirls in the mud after water receded. Autumn was his favorite season, with its shift from extravagance to subtlety, transforming colored leaves to brown, leaving the branches of the trees stark and bare, then drawing pictures on the sky when the wind blew the branches.

As a child, Luke felt ugly. When he became older, he realized that he was not truly ugly, deciding instead that he was only a little homely. Real ugliness, he came to understand, is rare, catching the attention in a horrified, almost shamed, way. But for the young, anything short of beautiful is ugly. Maybe it's just a lack of vocabulary at that age. When Luke was in fourth grade, a girl whose father had just been stationed in Japan arrived at their school. In later years her name was gone like the pictures the trees draw on the sky, and all Luke could remember was her black hair and a kind of prettiness about her. He became infatuated with the girl, but though he wasn't shy in other ways, he never had the nerve to talk to her. At lunch he'd sit at the next table over, never at her table, and sometimes in the hall he would stand quietly while she walked by. Eventually she found out that Luke was smitten with her, until finally one of her friends told him after school that the girl he liked thought he was ugly, and she didn't like ugly boys. Signed, sealed, and delivered notice of ugliness. He went that afternoon to an alley where he sat on a plastic box for a long time, until he was shivering from the cold.

Every school has its unattainable princesses. Luke was fortunate that he was not obsessed with his social position in school, as he preferred his classes. Some of his best memories of Japan were the field trips his class took, such as the day they went to Fujiyoshida, a town at the foot of Mount Fuji. It was a cold day, and for lunch the students sat in a steamy warm restaurant eating bowls of udon noodles, looking out at the mountain. Luke sat with Wally, and after they finished eating, the two of them started singing the song "Yellow Submarine". The teacher told them to be quiet, but instead they began laughing, until they were laughing at the very fact that they were laughing. It was in Japan that Luke discovered the Beatles from Wally. Both kids spoke tolerable Japanese at the time, and one afternoon Wally's mother came into his room and found the two of them sitting on the bed, looking at the cover of the Sgt. Pepper album and talking about it in Japanese.

In the sixth grade, the family moved back to the United States, to Carlisle, Pennsylvania, where Luke's father was at the War College. It was while they were in the states that Luke and his mother went every year to Charleston to see grandparents while they were still alive, along with Luke's aunts. During those years, Luke really got to know his cousins, Paul, Jan, and Anna. Paul in particular knew many cool and dangerous things to do, such as dropping powerful firecrackers into glass jars out in the woods, then running behind trees to avoid the glass shrapnel that exploded into the air. Another happy memory was of Anna telling stories on the porch in the heavy summer twilight, like the fantastical story about a woman who lived several houses away. Of course she was just a harmless old woman who grew an abundance of flowers, but Anna assured them she was a witch, so sometimes at night they would sneak out and go to her yard, where they'd hide in the bushes, thrilled by their own bravery, risking some terrible magical spell that would convert them into animals, or take them back in time, or deprive them of speech.

Just before Luke started high school, they moved again to Darmstadt, Germany. Maybe he was lazier here, or maybe the teachers weren't as good, but he found high school less interesting than elementary school. Perhaps he had more distractions. The interest in girls became far more focused than not talking to them in the lunch room. Nevertheless, Luke kept his grades up, because even as a high school freshman he was thinking about college.

One of the best things about Germany was making German friends, so that he became fluent in the language, and on into adulthood he remained in contact with Matthias. For a while he also kept up with Oskar. Luke had told his parents that he was riding with Oskar's brother to and from a David Bowie concert, and what would his parents have said if they had known that he and Oskar had actually hitchhiked, that they had sat in the cab of a truck while the driver told them about a prostitute he'd met in Bonn?

After high school, anxious but excited, Luke flew through the clouds above Germany, then across the Atlantic, to attend Georgetown University, where he wondered if he could fit in and handle the work. At first he felt powerfully homesick for a foreign country, wanting to go back home to Germany. At the same time, nothing could have made him return and admit failure. His heart burned with future success, which meant remaining where he was, studying, pushing on. Some of his freshmen classmates at Georgetown didn't know what they wanted to do and were simply going to school. Luke was one of the ones who knew, to get a job in the Foreign Service and go back overseas as a diplomat.

During the four years at Georgetown, Luke never questioned his drive to go into the diplomatic corps. Knowing his purpose in school made it easier to expend the effort to learn the difference between Romanesque and Gothic architecture when it was a beautiful day outside, or to write a critique of the Czech economy when reruns of Monty Python were on TV. During his junior year, he went to Russia and spent the fall semester in 1989 studying in Moscow. That was his first time in Russia, and while he was there he was all over the city, soaking up a sense of the place, not studying as hard he should have. It was possible to see that incredible things were happening. Hungary had recently opened up to the west, and while Luke was in Moscow, East Germany was full of protests (which were hard to learn about from the Soviet press), and in the Soviet Union itself, Gorbachev was in power. Instead of studying textbooks, Luke was reading this huge ancient city, as the people appeared to be waking up and lurching toward the modern world. One thing he also learned that fall, unexpectedly, is that sometimes you can be hungry and tired and lonely, and nobody around you really cares.

After his time in Moscow, Luke felt grand and wise, but he had not yet begun to discover the vastness of his lack of knowledge. In the spring after he came home, he met Aliselia Rosemiller, from Sylva, North Carolina. He was lying on the lawn near the Washington Monument on a Saturday, reading Dostoyevsky's novel *The Brothers Karamazov*, when Selia sat down nearby and asked, "Do you think

Ivan is crazy?" Luke said no, he thought Ivan was sane, so she asked if Luke thought the visions were real. And yes, he said, he thought people could have visions like that. Selia Rosemiller didn't think so. Luke learned that this interesting girl was a Russian Studies major at American University there in Washington. They talked that afternoon and then got some pizza, strictly pepperoni, before she went to meet a friend. That was the beginning.

Selia was cute, with wavy brown hair and dark eyes, but what Luke liked most about her was her interests and her desire for life. He also loved her sense of humor, which could be sarcastic, and several times he heard her say, "Be nice to stupid people. They control everything." She also swore that she found him attractive, and he could never get her to admit that she was only saying it to make him feel better. They shared a passionate interest in Russia and were both studying the language. Selia had never been out of the United States, but she badly wanted to travel and Luke told her real, and not entirely real, stories about his time in other countries: seeing a gym full of people in Japan all playing drums (real), almost getting David Bowie's autograph (also real), watching a bar fight in a cheap Russian bar (sort of real, maybe).

As he got to know Selia, Luke appreciated the fact that the first time he went to her apartment she had a large poster of the Beatles. When he admired it, she looked closely at Ringo and joked, "Isn't that Brian Wilson? I thought this was the Beach Boys." He was also charmed by the fact that when she really liked something, instead of saying anything she would just nod her head and smile. Luke also found that he could tolerate her negative qualities, such as the fact that she seemed perfectly contented if the kitchen didn't get cleaned up for several days. Or maybe ever. One time he refused to eat dinner with her because there were dirty dishes piled on the table from three days before, but in general they suited one another well.

He helped Selia with learning Russian, since he was well ahead of her in learning it. Sometimes he got frustrated if she didn't understand something, as he was not a patient teacher, thinking that the language should come as easily to anyone else as it did for him. Luke had also had the benefit of a good Russian teacher, as well as becoming friends with the son of that teacher, so that Luke occasionally spent time with a group of young people who spoke Russian, which improved his conversational Russian. Selia had had none of these advantages, but she worked hard, and she and Luke would sometimes speak only in Russian so she could practice.

After graduation, Luke and Selia drove to Sylva, North Carolina, to the little village in the mountains of the west, where she had grown up, and they got married in a Methodist church up on a hill above the town, with Selia in a white dress her aunt made and with a wedding cake baked by her mother. Just before graduation, Luke had taken the Foreign Service exam, which he felt was impossibly difficult, but he passed and got on the waiting list, a list that can involve some serious waiting. Selia and Luke remained in Washington, but they moved to a small apartment in Arlington, Virginia, for a price that was considered cheap by local standards, or expensive in most places. Luke was sure he would get into the Foreign Service, as it would be a mistake of fate if they didn't take him. While they waited, Selia got a job as a research assistant for a think tank, the sort of thing one finds in Washington, staffed with really smart, neurotic people waiting for the world to recognize how brilliant they are. It was called the Gaya First Institute, and they seemed to be deeply interested in how people around the world were using water. Luke spent three months working for a moving company, loading furniture, coming home exhausted in the evening with bags of hamburgers from Wendy's. He and Selia weren't earning much money, but they were young enough not to care, and they often fell naked into bed. On weekends they went to movies or to the park along the Potomac River, and they had friends over for dinner, as they experimented and learned how to cook with watery pasta sauce or dry, overbaked fish.

Then one day Luke came home and Selia handed

him an envelope from the Foreign Service. Inside the envelope was an offer of a position.

As soon as they walked out of the lawyer's office, Paul said, "Let's go get the letter." "Now we know where it is. Let's go over to Aunt Lindy's…oh, it's probably locked up."

"I've got a key," Aunt Maryanne said, and went into her bright blue purse.

The house was on East Bay Street, and each house along Aunt Lindy's section of the street had been painted in a pastel color, all the houses in various colors, so that this section of the street had the nickname "Rainbow Row", one of the more vague tourist attractions of Charleston. Paul drove down the peninsula to East Bay and parked on a side street nearby.

"I remember that desk," Paul said as they walked up to the lavender-colored house. "She said small mahogany desk in the hall. I'm sure I looked there."

"You're sure."

"I think I'm sure." Paul put his hand over his mouth and frowned in thought. "No, I'm sure I did. Maybe."

"When did she write the will, though?" Luke asked. "What if she moved it later?"

"No, don't even think that. It's just there." Paul unlocked the door and opened it.

They were in an entranceway as they came in,

which led to a longer hall. A small desk, a tiny table, and a chair were in the hallway.

"Is this it?" Luke asked, walking up to the desk.

Paul looked around, frowning slightly. "That's not mahogany," he said.

"What is mahogany?" Luke looked at the desk. "But this is the only desk here. Or is that it?" He went over and opened a drawer and lifted up a plastic bag of buttons. "Lot of buttons here," he said. "Several bags."

"It's not here," Paul said. "I know that desk. It stood here for years, but it's not here." He wasn't willing to be disappointed yet. "OK, somebody must have moved it into another room after she died. There must have been a lot of traffic through here. Let's look around." He walked off into an adjoining room, a living room.

"What does mahogany look like?" Luke asked.

"Mahogany is a dark wood," Paul said. "And the desk was about three or four feet wide, with three drawers on the front." He didn't see the desk in the room where he was standing, so he continued into another where Luke was looking. They searched intently, as if looking could make things appear.

For the next twenty minutes they went from room to room, checking behind other pieces of furniture, but that damned mahogany desk stayed hidden. Then they were back in the front hall. "Alright," Paul said, increasing his frown, "upstairs then." He was checking a green and yellow bedroom upstairs when he heard loud knocking on the door downstairs. He started back down and saw Luke opening the front door. A woman of about forty years old was standing there. She had straight brown hair below her shoulders, with a small chin and bright red cheeks. The woman was wearing a light blue uniform with tiny red triangles on it.

"Hello," she said. "I wasn't sure I'd find anybody here this afternoon. I'm glad somebody answered." She smiled and when she did her lips pulled back so that her gums became visible. "I'm one of the nurses who was coming by to check on Belinda, and I left a bag here. I was hoping I might pick it up."

"Oh sure," Luke said and stepped back from the door.

The woman came in and said, "I think I left it over here in the living room." She started toward the room and saw Paul up the stairs. "Hi," she said, "I just stopped by to pick up a bag I left. I'm a nurse who was taking care of Belinda."

She went in and picked up a brown bag by the couch. "Yes, here it is," she said.

Just as she was reaching for the door Paul said, "Excuse me, could I ask you about something here?"

"Yes?"

"We're looking for a desk that used to be here in the hallway, a mahogany desk about this wide–" He held out his arms. "–and we've looked all over and can't find it. Do you remember seeing it? Or the last time you saw it?"

She nodded and said, "Yes, I do remember a desk like that. I used to set my bag on it, then one day I heard it was sold."

"Sold?!" Paul exclaimed. "Who would have sold it?"

"About four months ago I asked one of the girls working here, and she said Belinda had sold it."

"Sold it?" Paul asked. "Sold it? How could Aunt Lindy sell anything? She *sold* it?"

"It surprised me too," the nurse said. "She certainly didn't seem like she was in a mental condition to be conducting that kind of transaction, but the girl said she had called up a man who came and picked up the desk."

"Oh Lord," Luke said. "I can't believe it. We get so close and then it's gone."

"I'm sorry I can't be of more help," she said. "But at least you know it's not here."

"Yeah, thanks," Paul said. "If you hadn't come by, we could have looked all day."

"You might talk to the girl and see if she can give you any more information. Good luck." The woman left.

Paul stood in the hallway a minute, scowling. "Damn it! Damn it! Why do things happen like that?" In spite of himself he had already started thinking about what he might do with the letter, depending on what it said, and farther back in his mind were images of Rachel moving to Charleston. "So close and Aunt

Lindy sells the desk. How could she sell anything? She was *senile*! Goddamn it!"

Paul went into the living room and flopped into a stuffed chair with a high back. Luke followed him and sat down on the couch. Paul looked around at the room, which was rather dark with the curtains closed. Framed paintings were on the walls, and a bookshelf stood to one side, not far from where he sat. Tall thin books stood on the bottom shelf. He sighed and stared at the floor, then turned his head back to the bookshelf, where he saw the titles of the tall books. "Gardening books," he said. He wasn't speaking to Luke, just talking out loud. "She loved gardening."

"Looks like famous gardens," Luke said. "Versailles. Monticello. Maybe she went to those places."

"Yeah, she and Aunt Maryanne went a lot of places."

"Yeah." Luke looked at the books for a minute, then asked, "How old was Aunt Lindy?"

"Sixty-seven. Not that old."

"You think she got what she wanted out of life?"

Paul blew out a long breath, then quoted a proverb. "Life is an onion that you peel while you're crying. I guess Aunt Lindy must've peeled some onions in her time. She never got married. But I guess it wasn't a bad life. I don't know." He paused. "Do people really get what they want?"

"Probably not," Luke said. "Not usually."

"So we try to enjoy what we get instead." Paul gave a short laugh.

"What if you get the short end of the stick?" Luke paused, then sneezed loudly. "Dust. If we could find that letter, would it help you get tenure?"

"Yeah, I think so." Paul sank his head back on the chair. "I think so." He sighed. "It would be nice to be more successful. 'Success makes a fool seem wise.'"

Luke said, "You know that George Harrison line about people who hide behind a wall of illusion and never see the truth? I feel that way a lot, about things in general, about what we go after in life. That we're chasing illusions."

Paul remembered reading lines from Rachel. She had written: "We don't really know what the world is like, so it's all an illusion. The only thing that's definitely real is the people we care about, the people we love. I know how I feel about you is real, that the light grows brighter when I think about you." Remembering this, Paul closed his eyes and for a second felt her in his arms. Then he shifted in the chair and sighed softly that she wasn't there, opened his eyes, and looked over at Luke. "Even if everything is an illusion," he said, "some people don't mind."

"I didn't say I mind," Luke said.

"OK, you don't mind. But you think nothing is real."

"No, that's not wha- wha-" Luke stopped and sneezed explosively. "Whoa! Didn't Aunt Lindy ever dust? I was saying I'm not talking about what's real and what's not real. I'm talking about the illusion of what will make us happy. Or the illusion that anything means anything." He sneezed again, then stood up. "I need to get out of here. Let's go have some ice cream."

"Oh, I could join that philosophical school," Paul replied. "The school of sweet delight."

Luke had naively assumed, in spite of what he'd been told, that because he knew Russian, and knew it well, the Foreign Service would send him to Russia. He was not yet accustomed to the bureaucratic logic that chokes all civilized countries. Instead, he and Selia were sent to ride the red dragon through Beijing. It was a wild change of life, from a small apartment in Arlington, renting Truffaut and Scorsese movies from Blockbuster, or walking down the street to a deli for roast beef sandwiches. Because he had lived so much overseas, Luke assumed, as though he knew, that the adjustment would be easier for him than for Selia. He was wrong. She was enthusiastic and threw herself into getting to know the new environment, the same way his mother had. Both he and Selia learned a little Chinese, which proved equally difficult for both of them, and after the first month it was Selia showing Luke how to use the subway. Once or twice he grew cranky—that is, dumb and immature—while she was showing him how to get around, when he felt confused and embarrassed by not knowing how to do it. "Yes!" he snapped once, stopping in the Dongzhimen station after she gave an explanation. "I know we need the yellow line." Selia grew angry at his childishness and walked off without him. He followed her, surprised to realize that he didn't actually know where they were going, aggrieved and humiliated. Besides riding the subway, he bought a bicycle and started riding a bike to work on Xiu Shui Bei Jie, where the embassy was located. He felt that being on a bike gave him something in common with so many of the local people in the city. At times, rushing along in those two-wheeled crowds, he felt like a part of the place.

During their free time, Luke and Selia were avid in exploring the city, and Beijing was one of those places where there is so much to do that it would be impossible to ever feel you had covered everything, even if you lived there for years. Some things would take forever to find, as well, in those labyrinths of *hutongs*, the narrow streets that are really just alleys. Luke and Selia did some wandering in the hutongs, and a couple of times when tough-looking young men were staring at them, Luke forced himself to bravely swagger past, not so much from wanting to appear tough in front of Selia, but out of concern that she would feel afraid if she saw him uneasy.

Beijing can have terribly hot summers and bitter cold winters, but in nice weather they preferred to be out smelling and tasting the culture of the city. One day Selia came home pleased that she had discovered a place to browse for antiques and jade jewelry, without the usual tourist prices. "I feel like a real resident," she said, and she was obviously pleased with herself. "Look at this." She pulled out a small jade dog. She never felt nervous wandering around the city. She had been visiting the Drum Tower and found little shops nearby, some of them selling junk, but there were more eclectic places, and she came home with the dog as well as round jade earrings and a kite shaped like a turtle.

During the winter they tried ice skating out on Kunming Lake. With a few words of Chinese and a lot of pointing and nodding, they rented skates, slid onto the ice, held on to each other, and fell straight down. Lying there, Luke looked up at a blue sky, at Chinese children who were laughing, and at their mothers, who were trying not to laugh, hiding their mouths behind their hands. Luke and Selia got up and fell down again. The children were as happy as a holiday. Eventually, though, he and Selia managed to slide around a little, enough to enjoy it. A week later they went back to try again, and eventually they became good enough that later in Berlin and Moscow they hunted out places to ice skate.

Life was fun in Beijing, and Luke loved the job he was doing. He considered it important work, in one of the most important countries in the world, and he hoped that what he did at the embassy would help improve relations between the U.S. and China. Sometimes with a translator he talked to groups of high school students, who always wanted to know about Michael Jordan. When they asked about him, Luke would pretend to dribble and shoot a basketball and they would laugh. All his life he had been aiming at a goal, and now he was there.

After the time in Beijing, Luke now expected to go to Russia, having done his time in a first assignment, but of course they didn't go there. Bureaucratic logic. Instead he was reassigned to Berlin. Although both he and Selia badly wanted a posting to Russia, they also loved being in Berlin, and now they were close enough to Russia to easily travel there on occasion. Since Berlin was in eastern Europe, and because so much was changing after the wall fell, it was a fascinating time to be there. Berlin itself had only become the capital again a few years before they arrived. Going to Germany for Luke was also like going home, to the place where he went to high school, where he first kissed a girl. He had been keeping up with his friend Matthias, and as soon as Luke and Selia could get away, they drove south to see him in Munich, where Matthias worked for a company designing furniture. Within an hour after they arrived, the three of them were sitting in an apartment looking out at the Isar River, laughing and imitating cats, which made sense at the time.

Later, when Luke was alone with Selia, he asked her, "How do you like him?"

"He's a nice guy," she said. "I see what yall have in common."

"What's that?" he asked.

"You're both sort of serious but weird in the same way."

"Weird?" he said. "Weird?"

She just laughed and said, "Don't be too serious about life, baby."

Matthias also arranged for their old friend Oskar to come down. It was with Oskar that Luke had snuck off in high school to see David Bowie, but seeing him again was a shock. Oskar was now in Hamburg, living with his parents, not working, and not looking for a job. "Why work when you can play all day?" he joked, but Luke was shocked and a little depressed by how irresponsible and lazy Oskar seemed. They had only been together for an hour when Luke knew they had nothing in common anymore, and when Oskar left to go home the next day, it was a relief.

During their time in Germany, Luke and Selia also made a trip, a true pilgrimage, to Hamburg, to look for places the Beatles had been. They went to Reeperbahn Street, where a visitor could still find as many prostitutes and drug addicts as might be needed at any given moment, or it was possible to simply visit the Sex Kino or the Peep Live Show. Luke thought it must have been the same as when the

Beatles were playing there, just as disreputable and frantic in the grim pursuit of pleasure. He walked around the city thinking about those scruffy Liverpool boys in leather jackets, wishing he could go back in time and see them. Selia helped him find the Top Ten Club, one of the places where the Beatles played, and it was still operating. Years later, someone told him the Top Ten Club had been turned into a Pizza Hut. It was painfully surrealistic to think that it was possible to sit at a table trying to decide about pepperoni in the same spot where John Lennon had stood at a microphone. How wrong the world can go.

In Berlin, they made frequent trips to Kiepert's bookstore, to see the selection of English language books up on the second floor. Selia was always looking for Russian literature, which she read in English, as she felt her Russian wasn't good enough to appreciate the original. Luke also read Russian literature, sometimes in Russian and sometimes in English, and they would discuss it. Because the American embassy wasn't far from Unter den Linden Street, Selia would meet him at a cafe there after work, and during their discussions she started to come up with theories about the nature of Russia based on their literature.

"They enjoy suffering," Selia said after reading *Crime and Punishment*. "They can suffer more than anybody else, so they can stand up to almost anything. Even communism."

"Nobody enjoys suffering," Luke said. "That doesn't make any sense that they enjoy it. It's human nature to avoid pain."

"But with our minds we can overcome our basic instincts," she replied. "Like choosing not to eat or have sex. And the Russian way of thinking is that suffering is good for them. So even if they don't physically like suffering, mentally they believe they benefit from it and don't try as hard to avoid it."

"Maybe Dostoyevsky thought so," he said. "But I don't think most Russians would agree with him. He was a writer, and writers don't think like normal people."

"But he was one of their greatest writers," she replied. "And that's because they read him. The Russians like Dostoyevsky, or they wouldn't read him."

"You're reading him," Luke said. "Do you enjoy suffering?"

Suffering was a subject that came up often, as they watched the frenzy of history speeding up around them. Berlin was an amazing place to be in the diplomatic service in the mid-90s. The wall had come down in 1989, communism had caved in almost overnight, to the benefit of the human race, and incredible changes were taking place in Eastern Europe. Germany came back together, Yugoslavia fell apart, and the year after they arrived in Berlin, the bizarre mad-dog Albanian government collapsed.

From Germany looking east, the view was intense. Working in the embassy, Luke had a weighty feeling of being at a turning point in human affairs. Sometimes he'd sit at his desk at the embassy and think, "My God, where is this all going?" Germany was dealing with increased pressure of immigration, not just the usual Turkish guest workers from years before, but now from the east as well, with Poles and Bulgarians and Russians. The other eastern countries had their own problems with movements of people or even deciding how to deal with people who had always been there, like the Gypsies. It's not necessarily good to finally be free to do what you want, if what you want is to beat up your neighbor.

"Yeah," Paul said. He was on the phone with Aunt Maryanne. "Yeah, people move around like that. Uh huh. Alright, thanks, Aunt Maryanne." He hung up.

"So you got the number?" Luke asked. Paul had called about the service that sent out the girls who stayed as companions with Aunt Lindy. Then while he was talking to Aunt Maryanne, she had gotten him into a discussion of friends moving to Santa Fe, because, you know, they had a son who moved out to Tucson, a lawyer, and they wanted to be close to him, but Santa Fe seemed like a prettier town, and they had been thinking about Santa Fe for several years anyway…

"Yeah, I thought she'd have it," Paul said. "She

doesn't know their names, but tomorrow I'll call, and maybe we can find out who bought the desk. You want a drink?"

"Huh, do I want a drink? Let me see. Do I want to drink more of your Scotch? Yes, I think so."

"'He who drinks and walks away, lives to drink another day.'"

"You know a lot of sayings, don't you?"

"Proverbs. I know proverbs. They add color to a conversation, don't you think?"

"Yeah, I guess." Luke shrugged.

Paul took two glasses and the Scotch bottle from the cabinet. "There's a show tonight on the history channel that I'd like to watch. That be alright with you?"

"What is it?"

"It's about the Victorians."

"You like the Victorians?"

Paul gave a slight smile. "People who thought they should rule the world? Who thought they were bringing civilization to one of the oldest civilizations on earth? What's not to like?"

The next morning, a Monday, as Paul sat staring at a jar of peach blossom honey, he realized they didn't know what time of day Aunt Lindy had sold the table. He dipped a spoon into the honey, then held it up to watch the liquid amber drip back into the jar. Without knowing the time of day, they couldn't know which of her caretakers to talk to. He pulled the spoon out and stuck it in his mouth. When he called the nursing service later, he explained that he was taking care of details from his aunt's will, and they gave him the phone numbers of women who had worked both morning and evening, Wanda Jones and LaTonya Hutto.

Before Paul called Wanda or LaTonya, Luke said, "I think it would be better to talk to them in person."

"Why?" Paul held the phone, ready to dial. "This is a lot easier, just on the phone."

"How bad do we want the information? We're more likely to get it in person. If one of them says she doesn't remember, she's going to think about it a little harder if we're standing right there. On the phone, it's easier to say 'Sorry, can't help you. Goodbye.'"

"Yeah…but if we say we want to come out and see them to ask some questions, that could make a person uneasy. Wouldn't it?"

They decided to tell the housekeepers that Aunt Lindy had left them a bonus in her will. Luke offered to pay the first bonus. "A hundred bucks," he said. "I'll pay it. We'll give them a hundred bucks and say Aunt Lindy said to give it to them."

Paul smiled and said, "No wonder they made you a diplomat. You can lie like Satan."

"We call it diplomacy," Luke replied.

Paul picked up the phone. As it was ringing he said, "If we have to talk to both of them, I'll pay the second hundred."

They went first to see Wanda Jones, who told them she'd be home that morning. She had worked mornings with Aunt Lindy, and since Lindy died only the week before, Wanda didn't yet have a regular job. About ten o'clock they arrived at the house where she lived. It was a small wooden house, painted pale blue, with a narrow covered porch on the front. Growing along the edge of the porch were hibiscus bushes, covered with enormous gaudy red blossoms. Wanda met them to open the screen door and invite them into the living room. She was a short, fat woman, with a very dark complexion, broad nose, and full lips. Her dark hair was plaited into small neat cornrows. She appeared to be in her early twenties.

"Hello," Paul said, "I remember meeting you before at Aunt Lindy's."

"You came by when I was there," she said. "You said Belinda wanted me to have something."

"Yes, in her will. She said that a hundred dollars was to go to you."

"A hundred dollars?" Wanda nodded, with a serious expression. "That was nice of her. She was a good lady, and I think she was a Christian even if she didn't go to church much."

"Well, she went sometimes," Paul said. "I just brought the money in cash. I hope that's alright."

"Oh, yeah, cash is alright."

He handed Wanda an envelope. "And I want to thank you for taking care of my aunt. I know she was difficult sometimes, and the family appreciates the care you gave her."

"I was glad to do it. Bible says we should take care of the sick, and I like taking care of people. It's a good feeling when you see you helped somebody." Now she smiled. Paul nodded as she spoke.

"If I could ask you one more thing while we're here," he said. "We're trying to dispose of my aunt's things according to the will, and there's a desk mentioned in the will that we were told she had sold after the will was made out. Do you remember anyone buying a desk?"

Wanda paused and frowned. "A desk?" She thought for a minute. "I only been working there six months."

"Yeah, we talked to a nurse yesterday who thought it was sold four months ago."

"I don't think Belinda could have sold anything four months ago," Wanda said. "Her mind be pretty much gone. She was done headed toward the Lord then."

Luke spoke up now. "We don't really understand how she could have done it either. But we thought you might know something about it."

"No, I don't know about no desk."

"Alright then," Paul said. "Thanks again for taking care of our aunt."

As they drove away, Paul said, "I need to find a phone so we can call the second woman. Looks like I'm gonna be out a hundred bucks, too."

LaTonya Hutto said for them to come on over. She lived in an apartment upstairs in an old house. To reach her apartment they walked up a set of outside stairs, with creaking boards and a railing that wobbled along the side. LaTonya must have been older than she seemed, because she looked no more than eighteen. She was a light-skinned brown woman, with thin lips and high cheeks. Her eyebrows had been penciled into thin peaks over her eyes, and she had straightened hair that was dyed blond. They gave her the money from the will, and when they asked about a desk being sold, she made them happy, telling them that Lindy had called a man to pick up the desk.

"She done it herself. She be kind of crazy most of the time, but then she do something like her mind come back. Like flipping a light on. Some man from over on King Street come by and got the table. He paid her cash, and she told me to put the money in a drawer. That money was still there when I left."

"Do you know what store he was from?"

"No, don't know that."

"There was a letter in the desk," Luke said. "Do you know if he took a letter out?"

"I think he looked in the drawers, but I don't know for sure."

"Well, thanks for the information," Paul said. "And thanks again for taking care of our aunt. The family appreciates it."

"Yall are welcome."

Paul and Luke started back down the creaky stairs. Paul grimaced as his hand shook the wobbly rail. "There's a lot of antique stores on King Street," he said to Luke. "If it's one of them, we might find who bought the desk."

"It's a goose chase," Luke said. "But I guess we can chase geese." They walked up to the car

As they drove off in a light sweat from the morning heat, Paul leaned forward over the steering wheel to catch the stream of air blowing out from the air conditioner, sweat running down his face. They passed a pale green, two-story house with plywood nailed up over the windows and door, and Paul noticed the porch sagging as if it was old and depressed. Next door to the abandoned house was another that badly needed painting, possibly yellow, judging from faded bits still clinging to the weathered walls. An old dark blue couch stood on the porch, and a man wearing long pants but no shirt sat there, watching the street. Grass grew high all around the house, except for a gravel track to the right where a car could be parked. Across the street from both these houses was an empty lot. Patches of bare dirt where children played alternated with clumps of weeds, and a bicycle missing one wheel was lying on the ground.

"What a lousy neighborhood," Paul said. "Why does LaTonya live here? Working people shouldn't live like this." He thought about the summer his mother had worked as a nurse's aide, how tired she would be when she got home from work, and the cheap apartment where they had lived.

"She could change jobs if she needs to get paid more," Luke said. "You go to school, get educated, and find a better job. That's how it works."

"No, it doesn't always work like that. Somebody has to take care of sick people. Should everybody who takes care of sick people quit doing it and get another job? We need caretakers, and they shouldn't live in slums."

Why would a woman who works hard and earns a salary live in a bad neighborhood? In LaTonya's case, a person might look at her and say, "Hmm, she's black, and she lives in Charleston. Maybe racism." A person might be wrong, of course. But since we have the information, we don't need to guess; we can look at the history of LaTonya's family. Obviously, if we go back far enough, all American blacks were living in slavery. Of all the ancestors living on the plantations—Tallboy, John, Vella, Mamielu—let's consider LaTonya's great great great grandmother Vella. She was a field hand who belonged to one of Henry Middleton's business partners, and she worked on an indigo farm, helping to ferment the plants to make the dye. Vella didn't live badly under the circumstances, but if it doesn't give you the creeps to think about a human being owning another human being, you need to stop and consider the state of your soul.

Of course, Vella lived 250 years ago, and we might

ask how something from 250 years ago could cause LaTonya to live in a bad neighborhood in an old house with a wobbly railing. As noted, we don't have to simply wonder. We can follow a chain of events, so let's jump ahead to see that in 1951, LaTonya's great grandfather Buster went to the bank to apply for a loan to open a hardware store. Even though Buster was wearing a dark brown suit that he borrowed from his cousin, with a red tie, the bank in those days rarely loaned money to Negroes, and he was turned down. So Buster's Hardware, with one counter selling sewing supplies for women, didn't exist, and the non-store did not expand to two stores under his son. Without the income from the two stores, it didn't even occur to anyone to send Jake, LaTonya's father, to Morehouse College in Atlanta. He would have become an architect, which we know because he mentioned that once to a friend during a picnic. In 1981, when LaTonya was born, her father was working for a landscaper as a laborer. Given the history of this family, we can't be very surprised that Jake had no expectation of his daughter going to college or starting her own business. Maybe he should have imagined more, maybe he should have thought of it no matter what. Sure, he should have. But we can't claim to be surprised that he didn't. Would we have thought of it? So LaTonya works as a caretaker for wealthy white women. Does this family history make LaTonya a victim of the past?

Is "victim" the right word? There was certainly racism involved in Buster not getting a bank loan.

"Life is filled with bad things," Luke said to Paul as they drove past a fast food restaurant. "We'll never make it perfect. Some people will always live in bad neighborhoods."

"No," Paul said. "I don't think so. I don't think it has to be that way. History tells me that we can get better. Our society doesn't do enough to give everyone an equal opportunity. We're tilted toward people who already have power." He remembered Aunt Maryanne taking him and his sisters shopping for clothes, but not all single mothers had sisters who could help them sometimes, the way his aunt had. "But things change, and it will. It won't always be like this."

"The government can't solve everyone's problems."

Paul frowned and pursed his lips. "Well hell. Is that an excuse to do nothing? You sound like a Republican."

"What's wrong with that?" Luke said, "I am a Republican. But I'm not making an excuse not to do anything. Government is a giant bureaucracy. It's the nature of it, it has to be that way, and giant bureaucracies don't solve very many problems. Everybody gets mad when they have to deal with a bureaucracy. I'll give you the ultimate example on Earth. Every institution in the Soviet Union, everything there, was the government. The whole country was a giant bureaucracy, and the country grew increasingly rotten until it caved in."

"OK, alright, but..." Paul turned toward Luke.

"We don't have a communist government. You know that's an extreme example. Obviously people need governments. We refer to places without a government as a 'failed state'. Complete chaos. There are things the government needs to do."

"Of course. But what kinds of things does the government do well?" Luke waved his hand. "That's the question, what can the government do well."

"What's your standard?" Paul asked. "That it never makes a mistake? There's nothing in the world like that. No church, no business, nothing. Government doesn't always work, but look how we've advanced through history. That's because we've given more and more power to more and more people, normal people. And they can only exercise that power through representatives. Look how good people's lives are in this country compared to anywhere on earth a thousand years ago. If you had been a radical who tried to change the society, educate more people, increase the wealth of more people, the conservatives would have opposed you. Right? That's what conservatives do. Don't try to change anything."

Working at the embassy in Berlin, Luke was constantly being reminded of the chaotic changes happening in Europe. If he was standing in line at a shop to buy Schrippen rolls, he'd hear two people behind him talking about privatization in the Czech Republic, and somebody's brother or business was thinking about investing. Another time he might be walking along the Ku'Damm with Selia doing some shopping, and they'd pass a newsstand with headlines talking about Yugoslavia, or what was left of it. "KLA Attacks Serb Village," "Milosevic Vows to Protect Serbs," "UN Urging Restraint in Kosovo." The war in Bosnia had just ended the year before they arrived in Germany, there was talk of war crimes, and horror stories were common about atrocities committed during the war. On top of Bosnia, almost immediately the problem that the diplomats had ignored was now heating up in Kosovo. Whenever the diplomats fail, the soldiers are called in. Being in the Foreign Service began to seem much more complicated in Berlin than it had been in Beijing.

In China the moral questions were so much easier—as much as the U.S. wanted good relations with China, there was never much question about who the good guys and the bad guys were. The government that had murdered its own people for peacefully protesting in Tiananmen Square was obviously a government that could not be completely trusted. Diplomacy in Germany didn't seem as straightforward as to what the right thing was. Serbs were oppressing Albanians in Kosovo, but the Albanians were also killing Serbs. If both sides are wrong, then what do you do? And the U.S. government seemed to want more involvement than the European governments, or less involvement, or at other times all the western countries disagreed. And weren't they the good guys?

"Why are you watching the news first thing in the morning?" Selia would say. "Why do you do that? Turn it off and have some jam. I bought raspberry."

But Luke felt compelled to keep up with what was happening. When he looked at other areas of Eastern Europe that had not leaped with red eyes into war, such as Hungary or Romania, he saw that what had looked like bright possibilities at first didn't seem to sparkle as much. The joy of a bullet through Ceausescu in Romania had faded with the reforms that didn't happen, and the Hungarians began to treat their gypsy population as subhumans. The excitement everyone felt when the Berlin Wall came down, when every human being with a brain that worked admitted that communism had failed, wasn't followed by prosperity or democracy. Where was the joyous future of prosperity and freedom that was supposed to happen? As a member of the Foreign Service, Luke came to see that diplomacy, even American diplomacy, was not about Justice, Truth and Peace. It seemed to be about what every country felt was best for itself. This was a disappointment.

He and Selia had many conversations in those days about what was happening in Europe.

"People are going to look back at the twentieth century as one long bloodbath," Selia said once, while they were sitting at the window watching snow come down. She had just been reading the *Herald Tribune.*

"This century seems just like all the ones that came before it," Luke replied. He looked out at the snow, peaceful and white and beautiful. "I don't see that much difference."

"No, it's worse," she said. "They got more efficient."

"I wonder if this kind of thing could ever happen in America?" he asked.

"We had the Civil War."

"Yeah," he said. "Once."

"Once was enough," she said. "They killed as many men at Gettysburg in three days as they killed in the entire Vietnam War." She was wrong about the numbers, but right in the general idea of destruction.

"The Civil War was not this century."

"OK," she said. "You win that point. I'll catch you on another one."

They watched the snow fall more, then Luke said, "It's been almost 150 years since the Civil War. How many wars has Europe had in the last 150 years?"

"Isn't it ironic," Selia replied, "that the Europeans always acted so superior to the tribes of Africa and North and South America? Like Europeans had risen above that and formed countries. But the Europeans never stopped being tribes, did they? All they are is a bunch of tribes with more technology to engage in their tribal warfare."

"The tribes are bigger," he said.

"Let's go walk in the park," she suggested and stood up. "Where are my snow boots?"

Paul was looking at a book he had left lying on the counter in his apartment, *Land of the Firebird*. A picture in the book showed a painting of Catherine the Great when middle aged, wearing a heavy green dress, with a small skinny dog looking up at her. "Catherine and her little dog," he said, more or less to himself.

As he sat down at the table, Luke asked, "What made you major in history?"

"Hmm, well…" Paul thought a moment as he picked up a potato chip. "I've always been interested in history, even in high school when I was thinking about studying astronomy. Maybe coming from here is part of it." He gestured with the potato chip. "I mean you're always running into something about the past in Charleston. But I guess it was my inclination anyway. Since high school I've been curious about the course of human events."

"When did you decide to major in Russian history?"

"I had one class in Russian history as an undergraduate at Duke. It was pretty interesting, and we covered some Russian history in general European history classes. I liked it enough that I decided to focus on that in graduate school. If you like a mystery that you'll never run out of, Russia is the thing to study. You know—" Paul reached for the potato chips again. "It wasn't until I was in grad school that I really understood why Catherine the Great is called 'great', when I understood more of what she did."

Catherine the Great. How many "great" rulers have there been? Alfred, Peter, Frederick…can someone be great without the power to kill people? Will people someday say Gandhi the Great?

Luke picked up a pickle and took a bite. "Have you read her correspondence with Voltaire?"

"Of course. I've read all of her correspondence. I'm hoping we might add something new to that correspondence. The Enlightened Despot. I think she was a lot more despot than she was enlightened."

"Do you? She brought reforms that nobody else had done in Russia."

"Yeah, she did. There's a reason they call her 'the great'—the first university in Moscow, educational academies, land reforms."

"And she ruled a long time," Luke said.

"Right," Paul replied. "As far as that goes, you can rule a long time as a murderous asshole. Take Mobutu Sese Seko in Zambia, as one good example. Nobody calls that bloodsucker Mobutu the Great. But how did Catherine really affect the lives of most of the people in her country? That's what I'd go by. Sure, she started a girls' school, but the condition of the peasants, the vast majority, got worse during Catherine's reign."

"I think she really did try to improve Russia," Luke said.

"I appreciate that. Maybe if she was Prime Minister of England right now she'd be fine, but absolute power isn't good for anybody." Paul waved his sandwich toward the jar in front of Luke and said, "Let me have one of those pickles." He pulled a pickle out, and holding it over his plate said, "The enlightened despot." He took a bite of his pickle, then frowned. "I don't like these pickles."

After lunch they walked to King Street close by. In this part of town, King Street was a pleasant business district, with many antiques stores, in some cases side by side. Not only was it a street with an ambience of leisure and acquisition, but it provided the pleasure of being able to go through other people's belongings. The only thing missing was the lovely illicitness of doing it in their houses.

"I guess we just go one by one," Paul said, shrugging. The store in front of them was called Janine D'Isabella. It wasn't large, and appeared to carry mostly glass items, but they entered and walked to the back, where a woman sat behind a counter. She had on glasses in large red plastic frames, her straight black hair was pulled back into a ponytail, and she was wearing a jacket of multicolored patches sewn together.

"Hi," Luke said as the woman looked up. "We're wondering if you could tell us whether you bought a particular piece of furniture about four months ago."

"Oh, I wouldn't know that kind of thing," the woman said. "I'll call the owner out for you." She stood up and went through a curtain, and in a minute returned with an older woman with gray hair permed up high on her head. The older woman wore glasses that she peered over, as she stared at them with bright eyes and a slight smile.

"Can I help you?" she asked.

But no, it turned out, she couldn't help them. They went next door to Low Country Antiques. This was a very large store with a lot of furniture, desks, tables, wardrobes, mirrors. There were beautiful and expensive pieces all around the large area that was like a showroom, and on tables were lamps, brass bowls and candlesticks, ceramic fruit étagères, and china bowls. Paul and Luke walked toward the back, slowly, looking around the room to see if they spotted a desk like the one they wanted. A long-haired man approached Paul and asked, "Looking for anything in particular?" The man's voice was soft and lisping.

"Actually we are," Paul said. "Several months ago my aunt sold a mahogany desk, and we're looking for a letter that might have been left in one of the drawers."

"I'll check our records to see if we purchased a desk like that. Do you know just when it was sold?" He walked back and clicked on a computer keyboard, desk, East Bay, Belinda Gildbridge, sorry. No such desk.

The next store was Quality Antiques, so filled with

merchandise stacked one item on top of another that it felt cluttered. They had only been in the door about thirty seconds before Luke turned to Paul and said that he had to leave. "This place is really musty," he said. "I'm extremely sensitive to mold. I'm already starting to get a headache, just from walking in the door."

"I'll talk to them," Paul said. "Just wait for me outside."

In a few minutes he came out, said the manager had checked their books, and they hadn't bought it either. "How's your head?" he asked Luke.

"Fine now. The air out here made it go away."

The fourth store was The Golden Cockerel. When they asked here, they were told that they'd have to talk to the owner, who was out until four o'clock. It was then just after two o'clock, so they went on to other stores in the meantime. With a surplus of walking around in the bright Charleston summer, however, they had no luck. None of the stores claimed to have gone to East Bay to pick up a desk. Paul contemplated their failures in tracking the desk with the letter, and he followed each gray thought to its darker cousin, until he had constructed an impediment to a happy life. He connected finding the missing letter with the book he was writing, which was connected with his getting tenure at his college. He had seen two professors, one in biology, one in sociology, who had not received tenure, though they had seemed to be doing well. From his own anxiety, Paul began to persuade himself that the future was murky, uncertain and frightening. Finding a letter that no one had ever seen from such a historical figure would surely secure his job. But what if he didn't find it?

After three o'clock they stopped into a bar for a beer, which was clearly overdue. After taking his first drink from the sweating mug, feeling the cold tingle go down his throat, Paul closed his eyes and sighed. The bar was cool and the beer was cold and maybe there was still hope in the world. Someone, after all, had bought that desk, and they would find it. He took another cold drink. God bless the man who invented beer. God bless him and his wife and all their sweet little children.

"Do you think these people could be mistaken?" Luke asked. "What if they bought the desk and somehow overlooked it?"

"I don't think so," Paul said and closed his eyes and sighed, then opened them and drank again. "I made sure every place knew where the desk was from. Buying a desk from Rainbow Row would have caught these people's attention. They're not going to forget they did that."

"Well…" Luke took a drink and said, "Ah, yes." He was silent a moment, then asked, "Have we covered them all?"

"In this part of town anyway," Paul replied, "except for the one where the guy wasn't in. I'm not sure if there are some antiques stores farther up." His thoughts went back through the stores they had been in, seeing tables, lamps, framed pictures, dishes. "There was a jade bowl I think I'll go back and buy," he said

"You like jade? I should have bought you some jade in China."

"No, it's for Rachel. I think she'd like that bowl." He remembered walking with her through crowds of people during the Spoleto arts festival, the first time she had come to Charleston. They had stopped to listen to a string quartet on the street playing Bach, they watched people dancing, and Rachel had danced a bit with closed eyes and a tranquil look, and they went into an import shop where she was entranced by the jade bowls. "Look how thin they are!" she had exclaimed. As the afternoon with Rachel had gone on, Paul had been surprised to notice that so much time could pass and yet feel like so little. They had only intended to spend a few hours at the festival, but the hours passed, dinner time came, and they were sitting together in a crowded, noisy restaurant. They had had no interest in anything around them, but with Paul's hand lying softly over hers on the table, they had a great deal of interest in their own conversation. How could it be otherwise? It was a fascinating conversation, with eyes that met, with hearts that went a little faster, with responses to questions that seemed exactly right. Paul sat there that evening amazed with wonderment, as the world began to fill with color and light and music.

How could he feel this way? He had barely met her. Yet he felt like he had finally found her.

When Paul and Luke finished their beers, they returned to the one store they still didn't know about. As they entered The Golden Cockerel again, they saw a man near the front of the store who looked to be in his late forties to early fifties. He had very curly hair, half gray and half black, with a graying mustache. As if to match his hair, he wore a black and white striped shirt, like a referee. He was leaning over a table looking at a book when they came in.

"Excuse me," Paul said. "We're looking for the owner."

"You got good radar, my friend," the man said. "What can I do for you?"

"We're trying to find a desk that my aunt sold."

"That's what we do here."

"She lived over on East Bay, Belinda Gildbridge—"

"Belinda Gildbridge!" the man exclaimed. "I've known Belinda for years."

"We're her great nephews."

"Pleased to meet you. I'm Tom Campbell." The store owner shook hands with both Paul and Luke. "I just read the obituary in Sunday's paper. I'm very sorry to hear about your aunt. Of course, she was real sick for a long time."

"Thank you. We were told that about four months ago she called somebody up to come pick up a desk that was in her hallway."

"That's right. I did buy a desk from her. She wanted to be paid in cash, I remember that. I don't usually do that, but since I'd known her for so long I went ahead."

Luke said, "We were kind of surprised she was able to conduct business. Her mental state was pretty reduced." Paul wondered if Luke had insulted the owner, implied something crooked on his part. But the man didn't seem to mind.

"She seemed kind of eccentric when I was talking to her, but you know, Belinda's been eccentric as long as I've known her. She seemed rational enough when I was doing business with her. You want to buy the desk back?"

"Actually," Luke said, "we're just trying to find a letter that was supposed to be in one of the drawers. It's an important letter that's been in the family for years."

"Why do you think it would be in that desk?"

"In her will she gave me the letter and said that's where it is."

"Oh. Well." The store owner made a face. "That's a sloppy kettle of fish, isn't it? I'm not sure if I can help you. Whenever I buy a piece of furniture I always check to make sure there's nothing left in it before I take it."

"Do you remember a letter being in the desk when you bought it?"

"No, I don't. I remember a lot of plastic bags of

buttons. I don't know what Belinda could have wanted with so many buttons."

"Then maybe somebody had already taken it out," Paul said. He sighed, then frowned. "It could be anywhere in the house."

"It could be," the owner said. "But I should tell you that a thing like a letter, something thin and small like that, sometimes can fall down inside an old piece of furniture and get stuck, so that you don't find it unless you're really looking."

"So it could still be in the desk?"

"I don't definitely know, so don't buy stock in that company. But I'm saying yes, it is possible."

"Then can we look?" Luke asked.

"Sure, but I should check my book, make sure I didn't sell it." The man walked to a desk in the middle of the room and took a large black binder from a drawer. "Let's see, it's, yep. Sorry, it's sold. But if that letter really matters to you, the couple who bought it live out on Sullivan's Island. Since you're Belinda's nephews, I'm willing to give you their phone number."

Finally, Luke and Selia were heading for the golden-domed, snowy country they had both studied so intently. They were going to Moscow. When the plane carrying them touched down at Sheremetyevo Airport, they turned and grinned at each other, children granted permission to use the toy box. They were finally going to live here, in the country of

Tolstoy and Catherine the Great, the country of Swan Lake and fairy tales about the witch Baba Yaga. If only they had known.

While living in Germany they had visited Russia twice, so some of their tourist impulses had already been sated. They had wandered in awe across the cobblestones of Red Square, with the high wall of the Kremlin on one side and Lenin's anachronistic tomb up against that wall, and on the other side of the square the huge nineteenth century shopping arcade. Communist mummy on the left, capitalist mall on the right. Rising up at one end of Red Square, like a structure from the fever dream of a dragon, is St. Basil's cathedral. At different heights and in various sizes on the church stand onion domes with swirls and zigzags of color. The church shows some of the manic imagination of Russia, commissioned by Ivan the Terrible, one of the maddest dictators the country ever had. This being Russia, it was a real contest. On those earlier trips, Luke and Selia had taken some of the usual foolish tourist photos of themselves in the middle of Red Square with St. Basil's in the background. Afterward they walked around the Kremlin, which is an enormous walled enclosure, then through one of the gates into that magnificent fortress. These are natural things to do in Moscow. Red Square is one of the jewels of the world. Still, there was so much to see and do in this city so morbid with history, yet a place so artistically creative it was like God's imagination. Now they lived there and could spend more time not only in the well-known museums like the Tretyakov, but also visit less famous places, like Chekhov's house or Lomonosov's laboratory. Naturally they took the train up to St. Petersburg and found the cemetery where Dostoyevsky is buried near Tchaikovsky, whose grave has sculptures of guarding angels. Before they went into the walled graveyard, Selia bought flowers for Dostoyevsky's grave, at a flower stand near which two women were begging.

As Luke and Selia passed through the gate, Selia looked at her flowers and said, "I didn't need to do this. Dostoyevsky is dead, and those beggars are alive. I should have given them the money."

Luke said, "Honey, you can't feed every beggar."

She stopped and turned completely to face him. "Luke, that's not an excuse not to help people."

Another trip they soon made was by train to Sergiev Posad, to visit the Trinity-St. Sergiev Monastery, the heart of the Russian Orthodox Church. Outside the monastery there were also many beggars, hoping for alms from religious pilgrims, who came here now that communism was gone. There were also groups of gypsy children, who might suddenly shove their hands into the visitors' pockets. Selia had brought a headscarf to wear into the monastery, like other women. People came here to pray and fill bottles of water from the fountain in the courtyard. Inside a monastery church, a group of young soldiers in army uniforms, caps tucked under their arms, stood in the packed crowd, listening to the priest recite from the Bible.

After an excited period of exploration, Luke and Selia settled into a routine daily life in Moscow. As with Berlin, Selia had no job in Moscow, but at first she was so pleased with the chance to explore the city and experience Russia that she didn't mind. After four months, she began volunteering at a battered women's shelter, a true rarity in Russia at that time, possibly the only such place in the city. Luke noticed that she always came home from the shelter serious and moody, to the point that he wondered if she should stop, but he could not have stopped her even if he had tried. In his own time off work, Luke searched out bookstores and began reading more in Russian, in part to improve his knowledge of the language, and in part to immerse himself more in the culture. It was in a café that he discovered he loved the poetry of Anna Akhmatova, after buying a book from an old woman on the street. From what he had heard about how the economy was affecting people, he wondered if the woman might be selling part of her personal belongings to survive, and he bought the book just to give the poor woman money. Then he started reading the poems in the café, difficult poems that he couldn't always entirely follow, but they had lines that kept him reading. "Отчего же Бог меня наказывал/ Каждый день и каждый час?" *Why did God punish me/ every day and every hour?*

Sometimes on the weekend he and Selia took the train for the day out into one of the villages in the countryside, to smell grassy fields, to pick flowers and hold them in bunches, or to eat sausages and brown bread with bottles of beer while sitting on the ground. It made them feel very Russian, as other people were doing the same thing, coming back on the train with bundles of flowers or twigs with colored leaves in the autumn. On those outings the two of them started telling each other silly stories about a family of squirrels, Mr. and Mrs. Belkin. Selia had a wonderful imagination for the stories, like the time Mr. Belkin became an inspector of foxes, and all the foxes grew worried about trying to please the squirrel who was in charge of inspecting them.

"Comrade Fox," Selia said, with a high-pitched voice that had Luke laughing just from the sound of it. "Comrade, I hear you've let your tail grow too bushy."

Luke jumped into her story and in a low voice said, "Oh no, comrade squirrel. Please don't write me up. It's a normal tail."

"I don't think so," Selia squeaked. "It looks bushy to me. We're going to have to shave it."

"Oh no! Oh no!"

"Turn around here! Give me that tail!"

When they visited churches, which they did often, in various cities, Luke liked the feeling of connecting with Russian history and culture, but Selia began to appreciate the churches for the emotional power of the icons. She could spend hours looking at the pictures painted on the walls and columns, on wooden boards that were hung all over the church, and of course on the wall of the iconostasis at the front of the church. Her interest in icons was becoming stronger than Luke understood. "Look at the composition," she would say. "Christ is floating above the void of Hell. And see this, he's inside a circle here."

They also loved going to restaurants, and one night they were having a pizza when Selia looked around and said, "This fat man two tables over, what does he do?" This was a game they had started playing in Germany. The idea was to describe people in detail and then decide what kind of job that person did. Because they did this so often, later Luke found himself studying people and noticing things about them even when he wasn't playing.

In the pizza restaurant, he looked at the man and started thinking. "He's very overweight," he said. "Wearing a blue running suit, not a very expensive looking suit, and white sneakers. Off white, they're old. He's sitting alone, eating a pizza. He's also going bald. Or he's mostly bald, just a little bit of hair around the edges, all gray. He's got a big nose and thick, heavy eyebrows."

"Like fur," Selia said. "You don't see eyebrows like that very often."

"And notice the book he's reading. Wrapped in newspaper, old Soviet style."

"Yeah, that's kind of weird."

"Maybe it is," Luke said, "but it's an old Soviet habit. Everybody used to wrap the covers of their books up with newspapers, so nobody else could see the titles. I always thought it was so if you were reading something forbidden, nobody would know."

"But if you wrapped your book up, that's how they'd know."

"No, they wouldn't, because everybody did it, no matter what their book was. It's strange to see him still doing it."

"So what job does he do?"

"He's a newspaper editor," Luke replied. "Or a bureaucrat of some kind. An old apparatchik." He pointed out a man in black coming in the door, for Selia to take a turn.

Selia looked at him a moment, then said, "He's fairly good looking, kind of scary, dark and sullen. He's wearing black denim pants, well made, obviously western, a black T shirt with no writing on it, and he has a silver hoop earring in his left ear. He's looking around, now he's talking on a cell phone. A gangster."

The hoodlum was followed in the game by a woman in her late forties to early fifties, sitting probably with her husband. She was not particularly attractive but had a pleasant, calm expression, and her hair was an unusual orange-red color, extremely popular at that time for dyeing hair in Russia. She also had a gold tooth in front, another common fact of Russian life. Because she reminded Luke of teachers he had had as a student in Moscow, he guessed she was a college professor.

"Oh, don't you teach at the College of Charleston?" the waitress asked Paul. She was young, with short straight red hair, and with a necklace made of tiny shells. Freckles spread from her nose across her high cheeks. Paul and Luke were sitting in Hyman's restaurant on Market Street. "You look familiar," the waitress said.

"Yeah," Paul replied. "I'm in the history department."

"I'm a student there," she said. "Are you Professor Gildbridge?"

"That's right."

"I think a friend of mine took one of your classes."

"I hope that won't affect our service."

"No, he liked the class." She laughed. "But it wouldn't affect the service anyway. Not much."

After the waitress took their order and left, Paul said, "You should come back next year for Spoleto. You just missed it by a few weeks."

"Yeah, I'd love to do that. I should come down and hear some opera."

"Oh well, I don't know about the opera," Paul said. "But there's a lot going on."

"Yeah, I'll definitely come for that."

"You'll have a place to stay." He paused and took a couple of sips from his beer, then said, "I told you I met Rachel at Spoleto. I said she lives in Richmond?"

"You mentioned that."

"I've been up twice to see her." He smiled to think of it, remembering Rachel's house, her jumpy little dog, her bed with blue sheets where they had lain for hours. They had talked about the Georgia O'Keefe paintings Rachel had framed on her bedroom walls. "No, really," she had said. "I always just thought they looked like flowers." Paul returned his attention to the restaurant where he sat with Luke.

"You miss her?" Luke asked.

"Oh yeah!" It felt wrong now to be away from her. Now that they knew about each other, how could the world be so wrong that they weren't together? Paul thought about the last time he'd been in Richmond, when they had gone to get ice cream near Rachel's house. There had been a street musician playing a mandolin, playing beautifully, and they had sat on the edge of a wall to listen. Paul put his arm around her waist and leaned toward her neck.

"Hey, don't put those ice-cream-sticky lips on my neck," she had said.

"Where should I put them?" he asked.

A young man had been walking toward the ice

cream shop with his daughter, a little girl around four years old. The little girl had long black hair, and when she and her father came close to the mandolin player, she stopped and began to dance. She had danced the way everyone should dance, with abandon, with joy, with no purpose in life but smiling and moving to the music. Later that evening, as Paul and Rachel lay talking in bed after making love, Rachel said that if she had a daughter, she would want her to be as happy as that little girl.

The memories of Richmond were laid aside when the waitress came back to their table. "Have yall decided?" she asked.

"I already know," Paul said. "I'll have the deviled crab dinner."

"I don't know," Luke said. "What's something good that's typically from Charleston. Charlestonian."

"Have you had the shrimp and grits?" the waitress asked. "That's Charlestonian."

"Shrimp and *grits*?"

Paul smiled happily at the look on Luke's face.

"Oh yeah," she said. "It's delicious."

"You never heard of that?" Paul asked. "If you want to try a typical low-country dish, it's really good."

Luke hesitated. "Alright then, I'll trust the two of you."

"If you don't like it," the waitress said, "I'll bring you something else."

"Alright then."

Paul's hair was falling damply into his face, and he brushed it back. His mind went back to a few hours earlier, when they were going from one antiques store to another. "The guy who bought the desk looked through it," he said, as though they were in the middle of a conversation. "He's been doing this for years. Since he didn't find it, the letter was probably already gone. Chances are somebody took the letter out of the desk before it was even sold."

"That's possible," Luke said, "Possible. Even probable. But we don't know for sure. I'm still willing to look for it."

"Oh, well, yeah. I'm willing." Paul took a drink of his beer and his mind drifted for a moment, then he concentrated again. "Well, you know, whoever took it out would have put it somewhere we could eventually find it. Right? Not everyone in the world is crazy."

"I don't know about that."

"It's not going to be inside a box of shoes. I hope not, anyway." He suddenly felt a hollowness in his stomach. "Man, we should have gotten appetizers."

"Yeah, I'm thinking that too. We did a lot of walking."

"Tomorrow we can focus more and look through the house."

"Yeah," Luke said, and looked around the room. "But if the letter did get stuck in the desk, that could get harder to locate. Already we're having to track it down."

"Yeah," Paul said. "That's true. Alright, then. We have the phone number of the guy who bought it."

After their dinner arrived, Paul said, "I'm still wondering something about Catherine the Great, if she was writing to Henry Middleton. Oh, but how are your shrimp and grits?"

Luke took another bite and nodded, then said, "Yeah, it's good. I really didn't know if it would be, but it's very good."

"Sure it is, it's low-country cooking. So anyway, here's an interesting angle I might use. If Catherine was writing Voltaire and Diderot... So she's writing these guys, who talk about personal freedom, I'm wondering how it would have fit in that she was writing to a guy like Middleton, a major slave owner who's also getting involved in a rebellion against the British government—"

"And about the same time Catherine was fighting a rebellion in her own country," Luke said.

"Right, Pugachov. And she executed him. She was defending her own crown against a rebellion, supporting French writers who are in favor of rebellions, and then she's writing to an American who owned slaves and engaged in rebellion? Very complicated, if she was really doing that."

The waitress passed by their table again. "So how is it?" she asked Luke.

"I like it," he said.

"Didn't we tell you?" She smiled and went on.

Luke turned back to Paul. "Middleton was a rebel, but against England. That might have been to Catherine's advantage. Maybe she was playing politics."

"Yes, I thought about that." Paul slowly shook his head. "That's exactly what she would do. This letter sounds more interesting the more we talk about it. Maybe our luck will change, as the proverb has it: 'Good luck never comes too late'. Or 'you never know your luck till the wheel stops.'"

"How do you know all those sayings?" Luke asked.

"Proverbs. I have a good memory."

"So do I, but I don't sound like Ben Franklin's Almanac."

"Neither do I. I just know how to add some collected wisdom to a conversation." Paul took a couple of bites, then said, "We've got a quest here. We'll be up against windmills next."

When they had finished dinner, Luke left the table to go to the restroom. Sitting alone at the table, with no conversation, Paul sighed. Suddenly he felt exhausted from running around all day, finding the caretaker girls, going to antiques stores. And there was the heat, thick and heavy with humidity, which they had fought their way around in all day. And of course he had consumed several drinks. Not that that was a bad thing. As he sat there, his mind returned to the last thing Rachel had written, and he recalled being here in Hyman's restaurant with her. That had been such a good weekend, when she came down. He closed his eyes and brought back how she felt in his arms.

When Luke returned to the table he said, "I almost got lost looking for the bathroom."

"Easy to get lost," Paul said.

Luke smiled a little. "I feel lost in the world."

There were days in Moscow when Luke would catch a troubled expression on the ambassador's face. The job did not look like something the ambassador was enjoying. But everyone knew that the difficulty of an ambassador's job depends on where they've been stationed. No doubt the American ambassador in London had more reason to smile about his job than the American ambassador in Moscow. For that reason, the ambassador to London is merely a friend of the President, while the ambassador to Moscow actually knows how to do the job. Soon after arriving in Russia, Luke emailed a friend he had worked with in Beijing, a friend later stationed in London. Luke wrote that he saw a lot of great potential in Russia, hoping that the U.S. and Russia could have good relations. His friend replied, "Maybe I'm just a jaded international bureaucrat who watches too much CNN, but I can't see two countries like the United States and Russia ever really being very friendly to each other. We're both too big and too proud of ourselves to be happy with sharing the world with another big country. We're like two elephants in a big open zoo, and while there might be room enough for both elephants, neither elephant is happy about having the other elephant there." Luke thought his friend was just cynical, not taking into account the fact that Russia was changing.

On occasion, there were things that Luke himself overlooked. With one of the disputes between Russia and the west, for example, Luke did not properly consider that Russia had emotional reasons to consider Serbia to be "their" area, and even if the leader of Serbia was a maniacal dictator and a cold-blooded killer, that didn't give anyone the right to touch Russia's little brother without Russia's permission. The fact that the Russians scarcely lifted a finger to stop the murderous regime of Milosevic in Serbia in some ways was not relevant. Right or wrong, Russia felt a real connection to Serbia, and as the tense diplomacy, the disturbing newspaper headlines about Kosovo, and the angry disbelief in the west increased, the idea of a warm happy relationship between the United States and Russia seemed like a fairy tale. The west was bombing the capital of Serbia. Russians were bombing the capital of Chechnya so that President Yeltsin could appear strong. There were days when Luke sat on a bench in Izmailovsky Park under a solid gray sky, considering who was right to bomb which city.

On Tuesday morning, a bright sunny day, Paul drove

Luke out to Foley Beach to see the house that Aunt Lindy had left him. He was still shocked to think that he suddenly had a house. If your elderly aunt died and left you, let's say, an elephant, it could be a shock. Even if you had a good elephant, adorned with crimson bunting and trained to stand on one leg while patting a child on the head with its trunk, that elephant was still going to need a lot of peanuts. How many peanuts did a house need?

As they got in the car, Paul pulled out a pair of glasses and looked at the lenses to see if they were clean, then put them on. "I still forget to wear these sometimes," he said. "I just got them two weeks ago. Aren't they stylish?" He turned to Luke and gave a wide grin.

"What are they for?"

"So I can see in the distance. I'm OK up close, but I'm blind in the distance. It's a very different experience to drive around and be able to read the signs."

"You weren't wearing them when you were driving yesterday."

"Yeah, I still forget."

"Well, everybody in this car is glad you're wearing them," Luke said. They drove for a few minutes. "What will you do with the house Aunt Lindy gave you?"

"I don't know. I could live in it, I guess. That would mean commuting back into town to work, but that might be alright. If Rachel comes down, that would mean more to think about, like how we can fix her up a pottery studio. What do you need for a pottery studio?" He stared at a sign in the distance, still surprised that he could read it from this far away.

Paul's new house was two streets from the beach, standing one story up off the ground, on heavy wooden posts to avoid hurricane flooding. The house had wooden siding, painted a pale pink, with dark green weathered shutters by the windows. A wooden deck, weathered into a light gray, also stood up on posts and faced the ocean. The small yard was mostly white sand, with bits of grass growing in it and with a row of short spiky palmetto plants along one side of the yard. Two tall palms towered over the small house. Paul walked across the sandy yard and put his hand on one of the wooden pilings holding up the house. They looked solid. He went into the shade under the house, then came back out into the sun. He looked at the bushes growing at the edge of the plot and scowled. "I think I'll cut those palmetto bushes down," he said. "I've never much liked palmettos."

"They're part of the local charm," Luke said.

"They don't charm me. Maybe you could spend summers down here and rent the house from me."

"Maybe I could spend summers down here, and you could let me live here for free."

"Yeah, maybe I'll just pay you to live here." Paul went up the stairs to the deck on the front of the house, checking the railing as he went. It was solid. From here he could see the dark blue ocean and feel the breeze coming in. He smiled to look out at the sky meeting the water, and he took a deep breath of the salty air. The inside of the house seemed in very good shape, but it needed painting just because the beige-yellow color was so damn awful. What sane person could walk out of the store carrying those cans of paint thinking, "Yep, it's gonna be nice"? He wondered what color Rachel would like, and it crossed his mind that maybe he should go pick out color patches and mail them to her. But what the hell was he thinking? They hadn't even talked about her coming down here yet. And if he didn't get tenure, would there even be any sense in it?

Later that afternoon they headed out to Sullivan's Island, to see the man who had bought Aunt Lindy's desk. Paul told Luke that he knew a wonderful place in Mt. Pleasant on the way, where they could have lunch. As they drove out Paul said, "Did I tell you that this guy sounded really interested that we're looking for a Russian letter?"

"The guy we're going to see?"

"Guy Hollingsworth." Paul laughed. "That's his name, Guy Hollingsworth. When I told him that we're looking for a Russian letter he really perked up. He and his wife took a cruise last year that stopped for a day in St. Petersburg, so now he says he's interested in Russian things. I'm not sure how deep that interest is going to run."

"How come you didn't tell me?" Luke asked.

"You fell asleep on the couch last night when we got back to the apartment, before I called. I forgot to mention it until now."

They crossed the peninsula where downtown Charleston is located and started onto the bridge over the Cooper River. "They have a race on this bridge in the spring," Paul said.

"That sounds dangerous. It sounds stupid even. What if…oh…you mean like a 10K."

"Yeah, a 10K run. Hahaha! You thought I meant a car race?" Paul laughed for a minute and Luke scowled, then he laughed too. Paul continued, saying, "It starts over in Mt. Pleasant and comes across both bridges into Charleston. I watched it this year, since I had some students who wanted me to see them run. What a bunch of lunatics. I can't imagine why anybody would do that, run ten kilometers for nothing. No beer, no money, what the hell's the point? But there they were, thousands of lunatics huffing and puffing across the bridges." He was now driving up over the Cooper River and could see ships and smaller boats out in the water, with the land lying in the distance in various directions, toward the mainland or toward the islands.

The restaurant Paul had in mind was on Shem's Creek, a fairly wide body of water. They turned off the main road and drove beside the creek for a while, as the sun gleamed brightly off the calm water. Boats were moored at docks along the creek, with tall metal arms sticking straight up toward the sky and with cables hanging down, so that each boat might have seemed to be a complicated array of masts and cords. In fact, these boats were powered by motors, not sails. The tall arms that might look to landlubbers like masts were part of the fishing gear for hauling nets. Paul looked at the boats and thought of what a nice photograph they would make. He wished he had brought his camera and wondered why he didn't just carry it all the time. A channel of water ran down the center of the creek, and along the sides were marshes, low thick grasses growing as if in a field, but the grasses ran on out into the water. On the opposite side of the center channel, beyond the marsh plants, were irregular lines of trees along the banks. There were also a few boats sailing down the channel of the creek, some with colored banners flapping slightly as they moved along.

The first lesson in being here

I WAS RIDING in the car with Paul, looking at boats on the water, and suddenly I felt as if I had been there before, in that spot, seen that very sight. But it was impossible. Maybe as a child I had been through the area, but this felt extremely familiar. And then I had a feeling so strange and astonishing I felt almost dizzy with amazement. I *had* seen those boats on the creek before. I had been standing in an underpass in Moscow years ago on a summer day, with crowds of people passing by while I looked at icons. This was what I had seen in the moving icon of the witch Bella. She had shown me this very scene, but why? *"You are looking for something, and I show it to you,"* she had said. But why was I looking for this?

They walked into the restaurant on Shem's Creek, and Paul noticed that Luke looked a little dazed. "You OK?" he asked. "The heat bothering you?"

"Oh. Yeah. I mean, no, I'm just, maybe I'd like something to drink."

"When we get something to drink, we'll both be OK."

Paul asked for seats on the deck next to the creek. "With all these shrimp boats going by, the fresh shrimp here are as good as you'll get," he said. "Maybe the best in the world. But I don't want to be too immodest and sound like I'm bragging about Charleston. Maybe they're just the best in North America."

Luke was staring out at the water. "Fresh shrimp," he said.

"You sure you're OK?"

Luke looked down at the menu. "Yeah, I'm alright. Just looking around. This place feels familiar."

"Maybe you've been here."

"I don't know." He shook his head.

Paul looked at the menu. "Fried shrimp, that's what God would eat if he ate seafood, and we don't know that he doesn't. My doctor told me to stay away from fried food, but maybe I need a doctor who understands culinary theology."

With their lunch they ordered beer, naturally, and when they had finished the meal they sat relaxed, staring without speaking at the bright water and at a shrimp boat moored near the restaurant. A seagull flew by calling out, and off among the marsh grass a white heron was looking for fish. "This is a great place," Luke said finally. "I could sit here and look at this for a long time."

"I love this place," Paul said. "I like this tin roof they have out here over the deck. It reminds me of that place we slept when we were kids, that cottage near Rona's house."

"Where we heard a ghost," Luke said. "I remember that place."

Paul smiled. "I don't think we heard a ghost."

"You've just forgotten. It was walking on the tin roof." Luke pointed up with one finger, as if the roof were over their heads now.

"Yeah, well…" Paul looked at the boat for another minute in silence, then added, "If you believe in that."

What if Paul is wrong and ghosts do exist? Maybe they're a kind of remnant of the past—a spooky, creepy remnant, but a remnant nevertheless. And if there are ghosts, then the past remains with us not only in the form of pyramids, porcelain dolls, and poverty. People say that ghosts are dissatisfied souls, lingering half in our world because of some misfortune they can't seem to get over. According to this theory, if you die more or less contented, you get on with it and head down that tunnel toward the light. A ghost thus reminds us of bad things from the past. Should we follow their example and hold on to the past, remembering all the evil that came before us? That's a hell of a lot to remember. But maybe we should. Maybe it's better for LaTonya to remember that in the past her ancestors were slaves. Maybe it's better for the children ice skating in Beijing to remember that their mother's older brother was gunned down by his own government at Tiananmen Square. Perhaps without remembering, we become like ghosts ourselves, incomplete and drifting.

Paul and Luke were driving past hundreds of hidden stories, moving toward sky and water. They crossed a bridge to Sullivan's Island, and in ten minutes had found the place they wanted. They parked facing the house. It was a large place, three stories high, a wooden house painted in white and light gray. The third story was smaller than the two below it and was centered in the middle of the house. The second story was completely surrounded by a large porch, enclosed by a white railing, and a flight of stairs led from the yard up to the second floor. Although the ground floor was enclosed, the house looked as if the real living quarters were on the second floor, similar to the cottage Paul had inherited from Aunt Lindy, and similar to so many houses on these storm-exposed islands. A small grassy yard fronted the house, with rows of palm trees on each side, and in the middle of the yard was a circular area filled with hibiscus bushes, now gaudy with giant red flowers, almost obscene in their display of floral procreation.

"Nice place," Luke said.

"Ain't it, though?" Paul replied.

They crossed the yard and walked up the stairs to the second story. Close up they could see even better what a beautiful house it was, very well kept. The front door was made of dark wood with beveled glass panes. Paul knocked, and in a moment a large man answered. He looked around fifty years old, with a thick head of hair, all dark gray. He also had hairy ears. His face was dark tanned, clearly from a great deal of sun, and he had a rather large nose.

"Are you Paul?" the man asked in a strong, loud voice.

"Paul Gildbridge, and this is my cousin, Luke Pharo."

"How yall doin'?" the man said loudly and shook their hands. "You called about the— about the Russian letter, right?" Guy Hollingsworth was dressed in a white knit shirt and brown pants.

"Yes," Paul said. "It's possible that it got stuck inside a desk that you bought over in Charleston."

"Right, right. Actually, it was my wife Carlee who bought it. You know how it is." He laughed happily. "I earn it and she spends it. I haven't had, um…time to look for it since you called last night, we're giving a party in a couple of days. I was waiting for yall to get here. She bought that desk for the boat, so let's go look out there." He closed the front door and added, "I'd take you through the house, but the maid is cleaning right now, so we won't bother her. She does a good job, and we're glad of that, so we don't want to irritate her. It took us years to find a maid service that really, you know, that really provided the kind of service you expect when you pay for it."

He led them along the porch around the house to a second set of stairs leading down to the backyard. The house was backed up against a marsh, and a dock stuck out into the grasses of the marsh. Several seagulls gave out their high, pinched shrieks across the wet landscape as the men started down the stairs. Attached to the dock and facing into an open channel of water was a large houseboat. The boat was two levels high, with the top level half enclosed and half open deck, and the entire boat was white with blue trim. Paul noticed that the name on the side was Amphitrite, which made him think of the word "dynamite", but he assumed the name was something mythological.

"Carlee, that's my wife, Carlee, um…isn't here right now, but she should be back shortly. She might know more than I do. Once in a while she does. Ha ha! I told her the two of you were coming by, but I don't think I made it clear what you were coming for." They walked across the wooden planks of the dock and stepped onto the houseboat. Guy Hollingsworth opened the door to the main cabin, and they stepped into the luxurious interior, which was a single large room surrounded by floor-to-ceiling windows. The floor was carpeted in gray, there were soft padded seats around the room, a bar was against a wall on the opposite end from where they entered, and a piano stood on one side.

Just as they entered, Guy looked at a vase standing on a table and said, "Now that's new. She must have just gotten that." He turned to look at Paul and Luke and said, "The desk is over by the piano. She's very fond of decorating. Carlee has a magical way of knowing what to do."

The Witch in Moscow:
"It's Cold Out Here"

A Russian witch might be called a "koldunya", which originally meant someone who casts spells. The idea of speaking the words needed to cast a spell is clear in the root of the word "koldunya". The root is related to words in other languages meaning "tongue", or "noise", or "call". This makes sense, because knowing which sounds to make is part of sorcery skill, a true fact in any language, with curses and omens and spells. The sounds have magic.

THERE IS AN enchanted transformation of Moscow when it snows. When the first real snow falls and puts a few centimeters on the ground, that enormous, noisy city suddenly grows quieter and more peaceful, with many of the sounds of the city muffled. The city that can be so gray and dirty will also sometimes look like a fairy tale. It's wonderful to walk around after a snowfall, when everything is still white and not yet walked and driven all over, and the snow is not yet shoveled up into clumps of ice. Walking in the quiet of a new snowfall was a kind of escape for Luke, especially when he strolled arm in arm with Selia, or when they stopped to grab up snow and throw it at one another. They would walk through muffled side streets, past the little churches with green roofs, hundreds of years old, that seemed so strangely located next to tall office buildings or ugly, blocky apartment houses nine stories tall.

It was January 1999, and for a January day in Moscow it was fairly warm, in the twenties on the Fahrenheit scale. Luke was alone out of the center of town, outside the ring road, where he had gone to see someone. It was still afternoon, not particularly late, but dusk was coming, as it gets dark early that far north in the winter. He was bundled up in a fur hat, which he had bought in Moscow, and a good winter coat that he bought in Germany. Luke walked along that day after his meeting, not caring much just where he went. He was in no hurry to get back on the always crowded metro, which would be even more crowded now with everyone so bundled up, to rush along underground. He passed a small park, where a kiosk was open selling ice cream bars, and a woman was standing at the kiosk buying ice cream. As much as he loved ice cream, he couldn't take to the Russian habit of eating it outside in the winter. Local people didn't seem to care about the season, they just loved ice cream. The kiosk reminded him of an argument he'd had the day before with Selia, when she told him that he ate too much ice cream, that it wasn't good for his health. He replied that he didn't need to be nagged all the time about this, and as an adult he could eat what he wanted. It didn't occur to him that real adults probably don't insist on eating like children.

Beyond the park he turned down another street, not a very interesting one, lined with the deadening masses of apartment buildings that the Soviets tossed up in every city in the country. Of course they needed housing quickly, but was their only choice really to make every building look alike, to make every building so ugly they make your heart ache, to build every building so badly that things didn't work the day the building opened? For this they killed and terrorized tens of millions of people? Still, in five hundred years, every single one of those buildings will be gone, and only historians will have a clue that any of this ever existed. Most people will never know there was a Soviet Union. But on that winter day, as Luke walked along, the fresh snow made even those terrible apartment buildings look better.

A few cars drove by with their parking lights on, the way Russians would drive, as the sun was then low in the darkening orange sky. There was such a pleasant quietness that Luke could hear his own footsteps squeaking on the snow. He breathed out thick clouds of warm air. Ahead of him he saw that on the ground floor of one of the apartment blocks there was a cheap bar. When he had just passed the bar, he heard a noise and looked back. Two men had come out, wearing worn fur hats and coats that didn't look quite heavy enough. The men were very drunk, talking loudly, cursing some common acquaintance, and holding on to one another to stand up. Luke stopped for a minute to watch them, and while he stood there one of them fell over into a pile of snow out at the edge of the sidewalk, shoveled up from a previous snowfall. The pile of snow was as tall as the drunk man, and he simply fell face forward on top of it. His buddy stood there saying, "Vanya. Vanya, get up." The first drunk didn't move, so the second one said, "Vanka! Vanka!" then clumsily grabbed his friend and pulled him up. The man who had been on the snow shook his head, and the two of them staggered off around the corner of the building.

Luke walked for a few minutes longer, until an odd feeling came to him that he was going somewhere. It was not a clear feeling of a real destination, just a sense that he should be going toward something, and he hurried toward the nearest metro stop. He got on the train still with the strange sensation, not sure what he was going to do. Only after the train had gone through several stops did he decide he wanted to go to Arbat Street. There was a store there that sold very nice embroidered tablecloths, and he had been thinking of buying a gift for his friend Matthias, who was getting married soon. Holding on to the overhead bars in the train, he rode to Arbatskaya station and went out into the chilly twilight, wondering if the store would be open.

The crowds of tourists who swarmed the area in the summer were gone now, though there were still people around. The businesses and booths that catered to the tourists were also gone, or else pushed back inside where it was warm. From the metro station Luke went into the underpass, so different at this time of year from the crowded noisy summer. He was hurrying through, hoping the store would still be open, when he saw her ahead of him. She had pieces of cardboard spread out on the ground, just like the last time he'd seen her, and the icons for sale were spread out on the cardboard. Bella was sitting on the ground, in spite of the cold, looking down, paying no attention to anything around her. In fact, there wasn't much to pay attention to. He walked up to her and stopped. She looked up at him.

"I was only going to wait another thirty minutes," she said. "It's cold out here."

He was surprised by what she said, talking as if they'd made an appointment to meet.

"What?" he said. "What do you mean thirty minutes?"

"I was only going to wait for you another thirty minutes. I'm nearly frozen." She sounded irritated. "I've got children to cook for."

"But you couldn't know I was coming over here," he said. "I didn't even know until a half hour ago."

She looked harder at him, and he remembered seeing those eyes, one green and one blue. "Why do you think I couldn't know that?" she said. "Do you want to see it?" She turned her head slightly and he looked to see the icon of the angel Gabriel in the red robe, the same one as last time, the one Selia wanted. "That's why you're here, isn't it?" Bella asked.

He looked at the icon and wasn't sure what to say. Had he really come through there to find her, not even knowing she'd be there? The one time before when she had shown him the vision in the icon he had had no idea what it was about and still didn't know. But wasn't this magic aimed at him personally?

"Yes," he said. "I want to see it."

"Of course," she said, and turned her body toward the icon. Like before, the angel began to move, slowly waving his wings until he was flying over the landscape as it passed by under him. And then, like before, he flew out of the picture, which moved faster until the image inside the frame grew blurry. When it slowed and stopped, Luke saw water but nothing more. The water was moving and sunlight was reflecting off the water, but there was nothing else in the picture.

He turned to Bella but she put a finger to her lips without saying anything, and he stopped. Then he heard sounds, but sounds that didn't make sense there in the cold underpass in snowy Moscow. He heard the sound of water slowly smacking against wood, the cries of birds, and the sound of someone playing a piano, some piece of music that he thought he knew but couldn't name.

"What is it?" he asked her.

"What you're looking for," she said, and like before, he had no idea.

A radio was playing on the houseboat, a piece of classical music, and Guy Hollingsworth walked over and turned it down. "So let's take a look in the desk," he said and walked across the open space of the houseboat cabin, toward the piano. "We should—" He stopped speaking and stopped moving. Paul and Luke stopped behind him, peering to look around him, wanting to see the desk. "Well, I wonder where it is?" Guy said. "I know this is where she put it. Saw it here a dozen times."

The cousins looked at one another, Luke sighed, and Paul closed his eyes.

"So it's not here," Paul said. "Well. Well. Why don't I feel surprised?" He had a sudden feeling that they should end this fool's errand.

"No, no," Guy said. "We've got it, she's just moved it somewhere. You know, she likes to decorate, pot here, table there." He looked around. "She may have moved it into the house. We have so much stuff in the house I don't, um…see where she could put it, but it might be there. Carlee always has liked nice furniture, even when we first met and couldn't afford what she wanted. She especially likes nineteenth century pieces. I'm more partial to modern pieces, stuff you can sit on. She should be back in a few minutes, and if yall don't mind let's just wait and ask her. I hate to bother the maid."

"We're in no rush," Paul said. "It's summer."

"Then we can just make ourselves comfortable here," Guy said.

They all settled into the padded chairs, and Paul looked out the window at the marsh, watching the seagulls swooping overhead. "This is a beautiful boat," he said. "It's nice out here."

"Thank you," Guy said. "We've had it about eight years, and we're pretty happy with it. We had a smaller one before this, but I wanted room to bring more people on the boat. I've always liked being on the water."

"Do you spend a lot of time out here?"

"No, not that much really."

"You really could live on this boat, couldn't you?" Paul looked around at the kitchen area.

"You could, and some people do. I don't know if I'd ever go that far." Guy laughed, but it wasn't clear what the humor was. "So yall are interested in Russia?"

"Yes," Luke said. "We're looking for a letter in the desk, from Catherine the Great. We're hoping it'll be there, but who knows? It keeps slipping away."

"Did I tell you that we were in Russia last year?" Guy asked. The reference to Catherine the Great didn't seem to mean anything to him. When he spoke, his loud voice boomed in the cabin of the boat, in great contrast to Paul's soft voice.

"Yes," Paul said. "You mentioned that on the phone. You said you were on a tour?"

"A cruise. They called it a white nights' cruise. Yall know about that? They call the summer the white nights up there because it doesn't get dark. We went to Sweden, Finland, Estonia, I think that was Estonia, and Russia, to St. Petersburg, Russia, for two days. It's a very interesting country."

"Yes, it is," Paul said. "I've been there a few times, but my cousin here has lived there."

"Is that right? You lived in *Russia*?" Guy turned in his seat and seemed a little astonished by the idea of living on that distant planet. "What on earth for?"

"I'm in the Foreign Service," Luke said. "I was a diplomat in Moscow."

"Yes indeed," Guy said. "Yes indeed. And what—" He stopped speaking and looked up as a woman entered the door on the end of the boat. "Well here's Carlee!" he exclaimed, seeing his wife. All three men stood up when she came in.

Carlee Hollingsworth was an elegant woman, several inches over five feet tall, in her mid-fifties. She had brown eyes and a small nose and chin, and her lips moved slightly at the corners, as if she was getting ready to smile. Her hair was brown and rather curly, cut a couple of inches off the shoulders, and she wore a black silk dress printed with a pattern of very large white flowers.

"So here you are." She came into the cabin, taking small steps, keeping her feet close together, almost a shuffling movement. Both her arms were out in front of her, bent at the elbows and with her hands hanging down limply from her loose wrists.

"Carlee," Guy said, "these are the two fellows I told you about."

"You didn't tell me *much* about it," she replied.

"I said they were coming over to look at the desk."

"You didn't say anything about a desk," she said. She turned politely to Paul and Luke. "How do you do?" she said. "I'm Carlee Hollingsworth." She held out her right hand with a limp wrist, so that each of them briefly shook her hand, introducing themselves as they did so.

"Luke and Paul," she said. "How biblical. I'm sorry I didn't know you were going to be here." She turned back to her husband. "Guy, as I was pulling out of the driveway, you came out and said 'Two fellows are coming by at two o'clock, and they're interested in Russia.' That's all I knew before I drove away." Now she turned again to Paul and Luke. "So what is this about a Russian desk?"

"They're looking for the desk you had here by the piano," Guy said.

"By the piano?"

Since they were standing, he walked across the cabin. "I think it was right here."

"Oh," she said. She looked at the two cousins, then added, "I'm so sorry you came out here looking for that desk, because we gave it away. It turned out it didn't really match the carpet."

"We gave it away?" Guy said, obviously surprised.

"I'm not surprised," Luke said. "I nearly expected it."

"But I don't think it was a Russian desk," she added. "I believe it was made here in Charleston."

"No," Paul said. Didn't this damned situation just figure? "We know it wasn't a Russian desk. It used to belong to our aunt, who sold it to the antiques dealer you bought it from. But according to my aunt's will, who just died—"

"I'm so sorry to hear that," Carlee said.

"Thank you." He shook his head. "But according to her will, there was an old letter from Russia in that desk, which she gave to Luke—" He looked over at his cousin, and Carlee looked as well. "—who reads Russian."

"Really?" she said. "That's impressive." She smiled at Luke and held her hand out, as if to emphasize how impressive it was.

"The problem is that my aunt wasn't in her right mind before she died, so she sold the desk, possibly with the letter still in it. We're not sure."

"Oh, well, in that case we could still find out," Carlee said. "I know where the desk is."

"When did we give it away?" her husband asked.

She looked at her husband, shook her head, then turned back to Paul. "My husband is a wonderful man," she said, "but he's not exactly carrying all the information he needs around in his head."

"I do earn a living," Guy said.

"Yes," she replied, "and I'm grateful for that. You earn a very good living." She turned back to Paul. "We gave that desk to Zoe Kirk two months ago when we took the boat down there. Zoe is a friend who lives on Ayaya Island, an artist." Suddenly Carlee turned to her husband and said, "Guy! How long have these gentlemen been here and you haven't offered them anything to drink?"

"Oh, I'm so sorry!" he boomed. "What kind of host was I being? And in this heat, too. Do yall drink beer?"

Luke smiled and said, "I think we can manage that."

"Is Palmetto OK? I think that's what I've got here on the boat. I like the local beer." He walked over to the refrigerator.

"I've never had it," Luke said, "but I'd like to try it."

"Yes, that's fine," Paul said. "I like Palmetto."

"Carlee?" Guy turned toward his wife, bent his head slightly toward her.

"Yes, I'll have one. Thank you, dear."

When they were all properly outfitted with a cold

beer, the way things should be, they settled down into the comfortable chairs.

"So you know where the desk is?" Luke asked.

"Yes, that's no problem. Do you know where Ayaya Island is?"

"I know," Paul said. "Luke isn't from here."

"Yes, that's right," she said. "You must not be, if you speak Russian."

"But I'm American," Luke said. "I just learned to speak it."

"My Lord, how is that possible? Did Guy tell you we were in Russia last year? He probably forgot."

"No, he told us."

"Well that language they were speaking over there, how can anybody make out that alphabet? I don't know how you do it. But anyway, if you know where Ayaya Island is, Zoe Kirk lives there, and that's where we left the desk, because she admired it so much when we were down there. The only way to get to Ayaya Island, by the way, is by boat. What kind of letter was in the desk?"

"A very old letter," Paul said. "Apparently Catherine the Great wrote a letter to Henry Middleton."

"Henry Middleton?" Guy said. "*The* Henry Middleton, from Middleton Place?"

"Yes, Henry Middleton was one of our ancestors, which is why the family had the letter."

"So you're descended from Henry Middleton *and* you speak Russian?" Carlee asked Luke.

"Yes."

"Well, my gosh, how interesting. You must be very anxious to find that letter."

"Yes, I'd really like to find it," Luke said. "We both would, but it's been such a frustrating search by now that I'm beginning to wonder."

"Oh, no," she said. "You're almost there. We'll just call Zoe up and have her take a look. Although she couldn't read it to us over the phone, could she?" She laughed happily at such a ridiculous idea. "Still, we could have her look."

Paul held his hand up as if he were about to speak, but Carlee continued. "Or if you want to go look at it, I don't think Zoe would mind. You'd need a boat to get there, if it doesn't bother you to be on a boat. It bothers some people."

"Oh no," Paul said. "I love going out on a boat. Anytime you're on a boat it's worth it."

"I'm sure Zoe wouldn't care if you come out," Carlee repeated. "She's an artist, and they're not like normal people, but she's nice."

Paul turned to Luke and slightly raised his eyebrows. "You want to take a boat trip? It's nice weather."

"Yeah, OK." Luke waved one hand to the side. "As long as we don't expect anything."

"Let's don't give up yet," Paul replied.

"Then I'll call Zoe," Carlee said. She walked over to

the table, took a phone from her purse and dialed still standing.

"Ayaya is beautiful," Guy said. "You'll love it."

"Zoe!" Carlee said on the phone. "Yes, yes, it's Carlee. I wasn't sure if you'd answer the phone. Oh sure." She stopped speaking and said, "She's on the other line." Everyone was silent for a minute, and then Carlee was speaking again. "Hi, Zoe. Yes, we did. How's Carmen? Oh, isn't that…yes, that's nice. I have two gentlemen sitting here with me—" She looked over at Luke and Paul and smiled broadly. "—who would like to come down to see you. They want to take a look at that desk we gave you from the houseboat a couple of months ago. It was their aunt that sold the desk, and they think she left an old letter inside. Yes. I told them you could look, but even if you found it, it's in Russian. You don't read— *Me*? You're a card, Zoe, a jack of diamonds. So these two gentlemen are also thinking that if they come down to Ayaya it would just give them a nice excuse to take a boat out. If you don't mind, and…yes, sure." She lowered the phone and spoke to Paul. "When?"

"Would sometime tomorrow be OK?" he asked.

"Zoe? Hi. How about tomorrow sometime? Yes." She lowered the phone again. "What about tomorrow afternoon?"

Paul looked at Luke, who said "sure", and Paul said, "Yes, tomorrow afternoon would be good."

"Tomorrow afternoon then," she said to Zoe. "We'll

give them directions. Oh, yes, their names. Luke and Paul, like in the Bible. Isn't that cute? Alright, I'll talk to you later, Zoe. Thanks." She hung up, then said, "She'll be expecting you." She walked back over and sat down again.

"It's beautiful down there," Guy said again. "It's um…really an unspoiled place. So you know the island?"

"Yes," Paul said. "Down by Kiawah."

"That's right. Zoe is on the south side."

"She's got a dock," Carlee said.

"Everybody there has a dock," Guy added. "When you go around to the south side there's a little bay there. It's not large, but it's the only one, and you'll see all the docks out in the water. Her dock is the second from the left, painted blue. And there's a path from the dock that goes right up to the house, pretty simple."

"Blue dock. I think we'll find it alright. Did she say what time?"

"Just sometime in the afternoon," Carlee said.

"It'll be fun," Paul said to Luke.

"Yes, you'll enjoy that," Carlee said. She took a delicate sip of her beer. "You probably should have offered them glasses, Guy," she said.

"No, I'm OK," Luke replied.

"How did you come to learn Russian?" she asked him.

"Partly in school, but also I got to be friends with Russians while I was studying, so I got a lot of practice."

"And you've been there?"

"Yes, I lived there for two years."

"So what did you think of Russia?"

Luke paused, holding up his bottle of beer. "Since I lived there, my experience was very different from what a tourist sees."

"Yes, I'm sure it must be. But didn't you think the Russians are unfriendly?"

"Unfriendly?"

"When we were in St. Petersburg people seemed like they were all in a bad mood. Nobody smiled, nobody seemed friendly. Except for the people selling souvenirs. They seemed nice."

"It's not that the Russians are unfriendly," Luke said. "It's just a cultural difference."

"It's a cultural difference to be unfriendly?"

"No, I don't mean that. But like the way Americans smile all the time. That doesn't necessarily mean we're friendly, it's just something we do. From the Russian point of view, we look goofy with grins on our face for no reason. No, I don't think the Russians are unfriendly, they just don't smile in public."

Guy went to the refrigerator, and coming back, asked, "You said you were a diplomat over there?"

"Yes." Luke tipped up his beer and finished it.

"I've been wondering something," Guy said. "Now that the Russians are a democracy just like us, why don't we have better relations with them?"

Maybe it was a natural effect of getting older, but Luke noticed in Moscow that he wasn't sleeping quite as well as he used to. He wasn't that old, yet in the middle of the night he'd wake up and be surprised to find a thought racing through his head, as if it had been going on without him. When he was younger he believed that when you sleep, you relax, your mind free of worries, but there he was, waking up thinking about work. Once he woke, he'd lie with his mind moving from idea to idea, as Selia slept beside him, snoring slightly as she sometimes did. Eventually he'd roll over, put his arm around her, and feeling her body against him, he would grow calmer and comforted. Snuggling against her, he'd listen to her breathing, his own breathing would slow, and he would thank God she was there. Finally he'd go back to sleep, and his insomnia was never so bad that it disrupted him from getting through the day. Maybe this was part of getting older. Luke certainly felt a lot less young during the time they lived in Moscow.

Friends from America, mostly Selia's friends, would occasionally express concern about the violence they read about in Russia. Luke and Selia, however, never saw any hint of violence, though they had Russian friends who said they had seen it. Misha and Margarita told about passing on the street after someone was killed, shot in his car. Everyone figured it was a gangland killing, a battle in the Mafia war that went on from time to time. It was a war everyone hoped to stay out of the way of. Although most people never saw violence, a consciousness of the possibility was a part of life there. Violence in Russia was different from the violence in America, as no one in Russia was afraid that they might be gunned down by an average gun-toting citizen who was in a bad mood that day. Nevertheless, the Russian Mafia were assumed to be everywhere, and in addition, people still remembered from a few years before when the Parliament and President had a contest of wills. The solution of President Yeltsin was to surround the Parliament building with tanks and blast it. Tanks were firing on the Parliament right in the middle of Moscow.

It should be no surprise that a leader who will turn the artillery on his own Parliament won't hesitate to smack his fist down on an ethnic minority if they get on his nerves. Yeltsin used the same heavy-fist approach when the Chechens, in a tiny area far to the south, began claiming the right to be independent. Russia was never going to let any area break away and become independent. If the Russian empire had to die, other people were going to die first. Yeltsin sent in the army, destroyed the Chechen capital, killed thousands of innocent civilians—and then watched guerilla fighters beat back the Russian army. While Luke and Selia were in Russia, the second war against the Chechens was murdering its way into the history books.

Luke might have said he began to feel wiser during his time in Moscow, but it was a confusing wisdom, a kind that doesn't seem very useful for anything except feeling gloomy. He could see that the great mass of people in Russia are normal people who wish their country worked—somehow—so that sidewalks aren't broken, so that buses aren't jammed with people up against the doors, so that the elderly receive pensions they can actually afford to buy food with. Luke knew that most Russians want a normal country where they can watch soccer on TV, go for a drive in the country on Sundays, fix up their kitchen with new appliances. They want this, but they don't have any idea how to have a normal country, and many of them are scared it might not happen.

One of the frightened normal people was Selia's friend Lyuda, who taught first grade. Selia and Lyuda were both interested in Russian church art, especially icons. They both had books on icons, which they shared, although Lyuda knew very little English, and sometimes the two of them would go off to churches or museums to investigate and talk. Their intense interest in icons seemed like a rather serious hobby to Luke, and at times he felt envious, as he had no off-work activity that evoked such a passion for him. On a Saturday in the spring, Lyuda came by their apartment before one of the church trips.

"Why don't you come with us this time?" Selia asked Luke.

"You two are more serious about it than I am," he told her. "You guys will have more fun without me there."

"It's a beautiful little church," Lyuda said.

"I'm sure it is," he replied. "All Russian churches are beautiful. But I'll stay here and work on the computer."

"That reminds me," Lyuda said. "Misha wanted me to give you his price list. If you know new people at the embassy who want to get hooked up at home, show it to them." Misha was Lyuda's brother, and several months previously he had started a business to provide internet connection service, along with a café, where he not only provided internet service for a fee, but actually sold pastries and coffee, like a real café.

"Sure," Luke said. "In fact, I do know somebody who might be interested."

"The more the better," Lyuda said. "He really needs the business. His krysha keeps his profit down." A *krysha*, the Russian word for "roof", was slang for "protector". Many businesses had a *krysha*, but it wasn't as if everyone starting a business went looking for one. These protectors showed up on their own, informing the business owner how much of the profits they wanted, and owners who wanted to stay in business paid.

"What happens if someone reports the krysha to the police?" Luke asked Lyuda.

"Who would be so stupid?" she said. "If you were lucky, nothing would happen, because the krysha would never find out. It's terrible. That's why I look to the past with the icons. I can't deal with our country's present."

Lyuda was right. For some people Russian reality in those days glittered with the light from crystal and diamonds, but for a lot of people that gleam was the edge of a knife. Not only were thugs leaning on the business people, but poverty was everywhere. Even in Moscow beggars stood along the streets holding cardboard signs. Some of the beggars were gypsies, who had always been there, but now they were joined by old women who had worked hard all their lives in the Soviet Union, to wake up one day and find that now they lived in Russia, poverty stricken with worthless pensions. At the entrances to the metro and in underpasses under the street, crowds of old women stood, ashamed, but with their hands out. There was also a third group of beggars, who made it more obvious that in some ways society had collapsed. These were military veterans from Afghanistan. Many had only one leg, or sat in a wheelchair with both legs missing, wearing their uniform, with a cardboard box on their lap to collect coins.

One day Luke passed one of the beggars in uniform on his way into the metro, where he saw a man in his late forties. The man was thin and had a worn-out fur hat and dark old-fashioned clothing. He asked Luke if he had a cigarette, then asked where he was from.

"I'm American," Luke said.

"You live in Moscow?" the man asked.

"Yes," he said. "I work for the American embassy."

"Ah!" The man's interest seemed to go up. "What does America know about us?"

Luke gave some embassy answer, but the man simply waved his hand. "You gave us this capitalism," he said, "and now the whole country is falling apart." He sounded disgusted, but with resignation as well. "Soon my wife and I will be thrown out of our apartment, because we can't afford to pay for it. Under Soviet rule, we put the first man in space and had great advances in atomic energy and science. Now look at us, people are sleeping in underpasses."

At the embassy there were people who thought this period of time was a transition to a free and prosperous Russia—an opinion that became harder and harder for Luke to share. When he looked around, he felt he saw a country getting richer for some, but not for most. At least they had freedom now, people said. That part was true. But would even that last?

On one occasion, Luke and Selia went to have dinner with Sasha and Louis, a gay couple they had become friends with. Although Louis was Russian, he said that Louis was his real name, that his mother had been in love with a Frenchman when she was a student. Louis also said he was named for that old flame, and that his mother convinced her Russian husband to use the name because she admired France so much. Louis was also very fond of telling dramatic stories, so a person didn't always know what was true and what wasn't.

"I have a terrible story for you," Louis said as they sat down to dinner.

"Is it too terrible for dinner?" Selia asked.

"No, it's just right for dinner. It's about Russia and we can talk about it. We're intellectuals, and we talk. It's part of our Russian tradition. It's all we do, in fact."

"Louis certainly loves to talk," Sasha said.

"What is your terrible story?" Luke asked.

"Do you know Andrei Khlebkov."

"No."

"Was he at the gallery?" Selia asked. "He wears black glasses?"

"Oh, yes, that's right. He's a friend of ours, Sasha met him in college. Andrei is a journalist, a very serious one, by the way. He works for *Argumenty i Fakty.*"

Louis did like to talk, and Luke saw that the wine was being delayed for the story. "Open the bottle first," he said.

"Yes, Sasha will do it. I have to tell you my story. So Andrei was on assignment in Irkutsk, to investigate pollution of Lake Baikal." Now Luke became truly interested, because he had been reading about Lake Baikal, the largest freshwater lake in the world, in the middle of Siberia. "Maybe you know that Baikal is still relatively clean," Louis said. "It doesn't have much pollution, in spite of our Soviet attempts to ruin it, the way we ruined everything else. Like the Aral Sea. Have you seen those photographs of the ships in the sand? But of course Baikal is nothing like that."

"Louis," Sasha said, "tell the story."

"Darling, I am telling the story. Andrei was living in Irkutsk for several months, investigating rumors that pollution was being dumped into the lake by several companies. I would say illegally dumped, but it should all be illegal, shouldn't it? This is one way capitalism and communism are alike. No one is responsible for destroying the earth. Andrei must have been doing a good job learning who was polluting the lake, because he made some very powerful people angry."

"Was he threatened? Did someone come after him?" Selia asked.

"Well wait, impatient girl, I'm telling it."

Then Selia got that suspicious look Luke had seen on occasion, head faintly tilted, eyes slightly narrowed. "Andrei didn't look like a journalist to me," she said. "Is this a true story, Louis? Are you making this up?"

"You're right not to trust what Louis says," Sasha said. "But I know this story, and it's true."

"What do you mean not trust what I say?" Louis turned to Sasha. "What does that mean? You don't trust me?"

"Yes, I trust you," Sasha replied, "but I mean you should have been an actor." He turned to Selia. "I know this story about Andrei is true."

"Of course it's true," Louis said, glaring at Sasha, "and yes, I should have been an actor. But let me finish. So Andrei came home to his apartment one day, and someone had broken in and stolen things. At first he thought it was some thieves looking for things to sell, but then he found a note." Louis paused for dramatic effect, as Louis would.

"And?" Selia said, giving him what he wanted. "What did it say?"

"The note said that his computer was at the bottom of Lake Baikal, and if he decided to finish the story about pollution that was on the hard drive of the computer, he would have to go to the bottom of the lake to write it."

"So he was threatened," Selia said. "He should have gone to the police."

"My dear girl, you don't know much about our Mother Russia."

"I know quite a lot about your Mother Russia," Selia said. It was clear to Luke that this comment had offended her. "And I know that if your journalists can be threatened like that and the police don't get involved, then you don't have real freedom of the press."

"But we know that, don't we?" Louis said.

Luke was reading a newspaper. He looked so intent that Paul decided not to disturb him, so he went back to his bedroom. It was Wednesday morning and they were planning to take the boat to Ayaya Island later. He brushed and flossed his teeth and found a cap to wear on the boat, then walked across the bedroom to his desk to look out the window again at the sky. The few clouds in the sky earlier had dissipated. He looked down at the desk, where his eye went naturally to a photograph of Rachel, one of the many he had taken of her. This one had been late on a spring day, the kind of day when the air fills with the sort of light meant for photographs and paintings. He had taken the picture as they were walking by the river, but in this picture the water wasn't visible. Rachel had stopped beside a couple of purple azalea bushes, wild with blossoms, and in the background, trees were exuberant with new spring greenery. But as Paul looked at the photograph, he barely saw anything else in the picture except Rachel. There was truly nothing in the photograph for him but Rachel. She wore a light sweater, of a muted rust color, which went well with the auburn hair that curled around her face and down to her shoulders. She was smiling, of course, but slightly, with her lips barely parted as if she were about to speak, about to say, "Why are you holding up a camera when you should be coming over to kiss me beside these flowers?" In reality she had said, "If we want to catch that movie, we should head back." Rachel loved movies. Then she smiled slyly, turned her head a bit to the side, and said, "After you kiss me."

From looking at the photograph on the desk, Paul sat down at the computer to see if there was a message from her. He reached for the mouse, still looking at her picture. When he saw that she had indeed written, he felt a sweetness so that his soul reached out to touch the machine that brought it. She told him about going to a gallery opening for a friend, writing, "Her paintings are almost entirely in black and white, or a little bit, you know, browny, like it got in there by accident. As much as I love Lorraine and I want her to be successful as an artist, I won't tell anybody but you, her paintings make me think of people in an insane asylum screaming. And Lorraine isn't like that at all." Rachel also told Paul about a cousin in Baltimore who "lives for emotional turmoil, it's kind of pathetic, like the time he started a fight with his roommate over who was parking in which space. I think Jack's constant crisis, or crises—his frantic life, really, spice up his dull life." Derangement seemed to be a theme for this letter, as she also said of her dog, Beany, that he was acting more crazy than usual, jumping straight up off the floor to snap at flies. It was a long email, and Paul felt happy reading it, simultaneously wanting to read quickly and consume it all, yet wanting to read slowly and linger over it. She ended with "P.S. Tell your cousin Luke hello, and I'd like to meet him."

What a wondrous thing to arrange the order of

strange little symbols, to manipulate letters descended from Egyptian hieroglyphics. Here is a gift to us from our blessed ancestors, who had the unspeakably brilliant idea to use random shapes to represent ideas and sounds. And how many kinds of magic came together now, for Rachel to be able to take thoughts from her mind, send them off across hundreds of miles, and put those thoughts inside Paul's mind? It's a staggering concept, if we think about it. But Paul wasn't thinking about the miracle of writing, of course. He was doing what he should have been doing and thinking about the sweet, wonderful person who had done the writing.

After reading the email he sat a few seconds, then stood to get ready by putting on a yellow shirt and green shorts, and he checked that he had his camera. He went out to get Luke moving and said, "Let's make sure we take some sunscreen. That sun can make crispy critters out of us if—" He looked at Luke a little surprised and asked, "You're not wearing shorts on the boat?"

"I don't really like wearing shorts," Luke said.

"On a boat? In this hot weather?" Paul frowned in disbelief. "You'll be a lot more comfortable."

"I know it would be cooler," Luke said. "But I'm not comfortable with shorts. You know I've got that birthmark on my leg."

"It didn't bother you as a kid."

"It did. Now that I'm older, I've learned to do what I feel more comfortable with."

"Oh. Well." Paul shook his head. "You ready to go have some lunch? You like barbeque? We've got the best barbeque in the world here in Charleston."

"It sounds like there's a lot of things you have the best of in the world here in Charleston."

Paul pursed his lips and shrugged, then grinned. "Not many places like that." He picked up the blue and silver captain's hat he had brought from the bedroom and put it on.

Luke saw the hat and said, "A captain's cap."

"Yeah." Paul laughed. "I'm the captain. You follow your orders, matey, and you'll have no problems. I don't want to make anybody walk the plank, but we're gonna have some discipline."

As they walked out of the apartment and down the steps, Paul said, "I think you'll like this boat trip. This will lift your dark mood a little."

"You think I have a dark mood?" Luke asked.

"You think you don't?"

After lunch they drove down to St. John's Island, where Paul knew a place to rent boats. Luke had already questioned Paul carefully, to ascertain that in fact he knew how to handle a boat, that this was not just a romantic prelude to death by drowning. They took a twenty-one-foot skiff, large enough to feel secure for the distance they wanted to travel, but cheap enough to afford. The boat had a small canvas top to help keep the sun from totally frying them. It was a clear blue day, fairly calm but with a bit of breeze.

Five minutes out on the water Luke asked, "Don't you need your glasses to see in the distance?"

"Not on the water."

"You're not going to hit another boat?"

"Trust me, Luke, I know what I'm doing."

Sunlight sparkled up off the dark blue belly of the water as they crossed it, the great pale blue arms of the sky surrounded them, and off to their right was the greenery of the land. They rocked slightly up and down as the boat skidded over small waves, and besides the noise of the motor, they heard the occasional sound of screeching seagulls.

Paul pulled out his camera and took a few shots of the land across the water. Then he turned and took a picture of Luke sitting in the boat.

"I'm not very photogenic," Luke said. "You're wasting film." After a few minutes he looked at the water and asked, "Are there sharks out here?"

"You worried about sharks?" Paul asked this while looking through the viewfinder of the camera.

"I just don't like sharks."

"There might be sharks." Paul lowered the camera and turned to Luke. "But since we're in a boat, they're not very relevant to our situation. Anyway, 'he that will sail without danger must never come upon the sea.'"

"I don't remember having any discussion about danger," Luke said.

"Can you swim?" Paul asked.

"Yes. I'm a good swimmer, but I don't think I can outswim a shark."

"Then if we fall in, you start swimming and they'll go after me. I can't swim at all."

"What!?"

They took the boat south, down past Kiawah Island. As they sailed, Paul rubbed his tongue against his tooth, where a piece of dental floss had gotten stuck between two back teeth that morning. He watched Kiawah as it went by, watched the beaches and houses facing the ocean, mixed with the green of trees and grasses. Toward the southern end of the island they saw sailboats out on the water, with tall curving sails. Most of the sails were white, but one boat had dark red sails, the color of wine. He got the camera out again and zoomed in on the wine-dark sails.

"Hey!" Luke said to Paul. "Could we turn off the motor and sit for a few minutes?"

Paul said nothing, but reached over to the motor, and as the sound died they could suddenly hear seagulls and waves slapping their boat. They sat silently for a bit, rocking on the water, watching the arched sails move across the water.

"Have you come out in a boat very often?" Luke asked.

"I wouldn't call it often. Enough to know what I'm doing. The last time Rachel was here we wanted to go out, but we didn't manage it."

They sat in silence again, rocking up and down with the waves. A gull floated over them, tipping its wings slightly back and forth. Paul lifted his camera and took a picture of the bird.

"You're going to ask her to move, aren't you?" Luke asked.

"I think she'll fly away by herself."

"I don't mean the seagull."

Paul looked at him.

"Rachel. Aren't you going to ask her to move down here?"

"You know I'm waiting to hear about tenure." Paul lifted the camera again and looked out at the water.

"Why? Why wait?"

"For security." Paul lowered the camera and turned back to Luke. "So she doesn't move down here for nothing."

Luke looked quizzical. "How can it be for nothing if you're here?"

"If I don't get tenure, we might have to move, so she'd be moving again."

"So what? People do." Again they sat silently. "I can see you're in love with her," Luke said. "You should be together."

Paul looked at his cousin and pulled his sunglasses down on his nose, to look over them. "How can you see it?"

For a second Luke didn't reply, then he said, "I

know what it's like to be in love. When you find the right person, don't let her disappear."

"I'm not going to let her disappear." Paul tried to drop the subject, as it touched an uncomfortable spot for him. He wanted more than anything for Rachel to be here, but he was unsure what to do. He lifted the camera again, looked through it and took another picture. When he did so the roll of film came to an end and began to automatically rewind.

While Paul was changing the film, Luke said, "Tell me something about this guy Catherine wrote to. Our ancestor. Was he really our ancestor?"

"Yep." Paul had a new roll of film in the camera and snapped the cover back in place.

"And he was president of the Continental Congress?"

"He was President of the first one. There were two of them. And it's probably not as impressive as it sounds. The guy who served as president for most of the congress resigned to go back to Virginia, and then Henry Middleton was elected president for four days, until it ended."

"No," Luke said. "It doesn't sound quite the same when you have the details."

"But even so, there were a lot of men there, and he was the one they chose. He was also a powerful man down here in South Carolina. He owned more than 50,000 acres of land and around 800 slaves."

"Mr. Liberty."

"Yeah, the irony is fantastic," Paul said. "But people who are really rich are always interesting. They can turn every whim into physical reality. I told you, right, that you can still visit his estate? It's out at Middleton Place."

"You mentioned that. Guy Hollingsworth mentioned that name, too."

"But that was from his wife's family. After Henry's wife died, he gave Middleton Place to his son, Arthur. Arthur was elected to the Second Continental Congress and signed the Declaration of Independence."

Luke did a quick jerk of the head. "I have an ancestor who signed the Declaration?"

"I told you, it's an interesting family, until it gets to us. But here's the part you'll really like. Arthur's son was also Henry, and Henry number two was later the American Minister to Russia, basically the ambassador. So you and Henry number two have both worked as diplomats in Russia."

"Well my God." Luke looked astonished and delighted by this information. "How come you didn't tell me this before?"

"I don't know." Paul raised his eyebrows and did a quick smile. "I've been thinking about other things."

"So did this second Henry Middleton speak Russian? I guess he must have."

"After ten years over there you'd think so, but I don't know." Paul held the camera again to his eye.

"Smile for the future." He turned the camera toward Luke.

Luke ignored him and said, "The ambassador to Russia. I'd like to go out and see Middleton Place."

Paul took a photo, then lowered the camera. "We could do that. It's not the same as in Middleton's day, though. Most of the house got burned down during the Civil War, and then some of what was left got knocked down by the earthquake. But one wing is still standing, and you get some sense of history."

Luke nodded slowly. "Yeah, I'd like to do that."

The sailboats had moved away from them now, cutting around the edge of the island.

"We'd better get on down there," Paul said. "She's expecting us."

"Zoe Kirk," Luke said, clearly enunciating her name as if he were practicing it.

Paul started the motor, and the front of the boat raised up slightly as they started forward again. With their movement came a welcome breeze.

Ayaya Island was fairly small, just south of Kiawah. From their first view of it, Ayaya seemed deserted, with a beautiful but empty beach, and behind the beach, palm trees were mixed with oaks. Following Guy Hollingsworth's directions, Paul directed their boat to the south side, where a small inlet opened up. They saw six or seven docks out in the water of the inlet, with a boat at every dock, and the second dock from the left, as Guy had said, was blue.

The second lesson
in being here

I WAS SAILING with Paul to Ayaya Island in the Charleston bay, going to see Zoe Kirk. It was a beautiful sunny day and I felt relaxed. When we got to the island, Paul was maneuvering the boat up to the dock, and I was looking down at the water. I could hear seagulls or some kind of bird, and I watched the water smacking against the side of our boat. And then I heard a piano playing, something by Chopin, but I didn't know the name. The birds, the water, the music—suddenly, I realized that this was the combination of sounds I had experienced with the witch Bella, back in Moscow. I had stood in that dark winter underpass, looking down at her icon, and I had heard these birds, this music. "This is what you're looking for," she said.

As they turned off the motor and drifted up to the dock, they heard a piano in a nearby house. From the blue dock, a path made of crushed shells led up to the house, a building that stood out because it was made of stone. The other few houses that were visible were all of wooden construction. Zoe Kirk's stone house was mostly a one-story place, but on one end there was a second story with large windows.

Paul tied their boat up to the dock and looked around at the small inlet. "I wonder who's playing the piano?" He looked over at Luke, who was staring toward Zoe's house. "Do you know that piece?" Paul asked, but Luke didn't answer.

They started up the short path to the house, and when they were halfway there a woman came out to meet them. She wore a long white dress, soft and flowing around the shape of her body. The bright whiteness of the dress set off the dark brown tone of her skin. Her hair was slightly reddish and very curly, and as she came she looked to be in her mid-forties. She had full lips, very dark brown eyes, and thin eyebrows.

"Luke and Paul?" she said.

"Yes," Paul said. "You're Zoe Kirk?"

"That's right. Carlee said yall wanted to see the desk she gave me."

"Yeah," Paul said. "We do, though I guess I was also looking for an excuse to take my cousin out on the water. I'm Paul." He shook Zoe's hand, which she held toward him.

"Luke Pharo," Luke said, and also shook her hand.

"It can be nice to go out in a boat," she said. "Although living here on this island, we sometimes do more of it than we want to." She smiled so brightly that it was hard to believe it really concerned her to have to use a boat.

"My cousin Luke is just visiting Charleston for a few days, and I also wanted him to experience more than walking around in town." Paul nodded toward Luke, who smiled when Zoe turned toward him.

"Definitely," Zoe said, apparently to Luke. "To appreciate Charleston, I think you have to get out of the city. Come on up to the house and I'll show you the desk." All the time they had been talking, the piano had continued to play. As they approached the house, Zoe said, "That's my daughter, Carmen, on the piano. She just graduated from Indiana University with a degree in music. Her main instrument is violin, but I think she's very good on the piano." They stopped just outside the front door. Carmen was indeed very good.

"She's home for a couple of weeks, but she's about to take a job with the symphony in Philadelphia." Zoe turned back and opened the front door. It was cooler in the stone house, out of the sun. There was no air conditioning, but the windows were open and a breeze blew through.

"So let me show you the desk," Zoe said. The big room where they first entered had bare stone walls, but was hung with large paintings. Also sitting around the room, on tables and on the floor, were many baskets.

"I put the desk in my studio," Zoe said. "It's

upstairs. I get a lot of light up there." A fairly wide set of wooden stairs led up to the second story.

Paul looked at the paintings hanging around the room, renditions of marshes, beaches, islands, some of the things he really liked about this area, some of the things he took photographs of himself. The paintings were all in a similar style, and he guessed that they must be Zoe's pictures. He liked them. Every image had blue in it, and they were all filled with light. Luke, too, was looking at the paintings, and he said, "Are these yours? I love these. This is the kind of style that really appeals to me."

"Thank you," Zoe said. "They're all mine except the one on that wall."

The three of them went up to the second floor, to a single room almost completely surrounded by windows. Three easels stood with canvases on them, one canvas blank and white, the other two appearing finished. Stacks of other paintings were leaned up against the windows; there was a sink on one side and a couch against a window. The couch was yellow but had collected a mottled splattering of paint.

"Here it is," Zoe said, pointing out the desk beside the couch.

Paul walked toward the desk, then stopped. "That's not the desk."

"What?" Zoe asked, confused. "This is the desk that Carlee had on the boat. Weren't you looking for this?"

"We're looking for a desk that belonged to our aunt," he said. "She sold it to a store on King Street and…" He stopped and let out a breath.

"Carlee said she bought this on King Street."

He pursed his lips for a second. "It's a different desk, though. The owner of the store must have made a mistake. He sent us after the wrong desk."

Luke closed his eyes and put his head in his hand for a second. Then he opened his eyes and said, "No desk. No letter." He smiled a resigned smile, then looked over at Paul and shrugged slightly. "But at least we got a boat ride. And you were right. That was pretty nice."

"Yep," Paul said. "But no letter."

Zoe said. "I'm really sorry that you came all this way, and this isn't the desk you were looking for."

"But what happened to the desk?" Luke asked, frowning slightly.

Paul wondered how in the world they had so carefully followed a dead end. How many links in this chain to nowhere? Oh well… The philosopher Mick Jagger came to mind. *You can't always get what you want.* He turned to Zoe. "I like what you paint. I like to take photographs of the same types of things. Your pictures have a nice feel for the area."

"I try to," she said. "I'm from Charleston, born on the islands. I'm a child of the sky and the sea, and I like trying to paint it." She looked at several of the paintings there in the studio, then seemed to study one of them. "Someday I'm hoping to finally paint a picture that seems completely right to me."

"I suppose artists are never really satisfied with their own work," Luke said.

"No, I don't think artists are," she said, still looking at her paintings. "Because with art you're trying to say something that can't really be said."

"That's true with words too," Luke said. "Sometimes words don't work."

"I suppose so," she replied. Then she turned to Luke. "There are people who call themselves artists who are satisfied with what they do, but I think if you're a real artist, you're always reaching but never quite touch it." She closed her eyes for a second, then opened them again.

While Zoe and Luke were speaking, Paul was walking around looking at the pictures. "Do you always do landscape subjects?" he asked. He was standing in front of one of the easels. The painting showed a flowering bush with the sun on it in late afternoon. Paul turned back around and out the window saw Zoe's daughter, Carmen, headed down the path to the dock.

"Mostly," Zoe said. "I do have a few in another style that I do partly for fun and partly because they bring in more money." She walked over to another stack of canvases and began pulling several out, standing them out for view. These all showed anthropomorphic pigs, dressed like people, in various human situations.

There was a group of pigs standing at a pig bar holding beers. Here were pigs playing golf, pigs at the pig hardware store, a pig under arrest standing before a pig judge. One picture showed two pigs floating in a hot air balloon.

Paul laughed and said, "All the pigs are men."

"I was married for a while," Zoe said and laughed as well. "That might explain that. But people buy them."

"These two pigs are floating across India," Luke said, looking at the balloon picture.

"Oh, I read about that," Zoe said. "There's two people crossing the country and tossing out drawings of doves."

"Your paintings remind me of the Beatles' song Piggies." Luke started to sing it, and sang surprisingly well. "Everywhere there's lots of piggies, living piggy lives. You can see them out for dinner with their piggy wives." He stopped singing. "Except no piggy wives here."

"How strange," Zoe said, looking at her paintings. "I never thought about that song while I was doing these." She looked at the pictures for a few seconds. "Never even entered my head. Now I'll think about it every time." Then she turned toward the stairs. "Well, even though yall made a trip for nothing, I'd like to at least offer you something to eat and drink."

"Sounds good to me," Paul said and nodded.

They went back downstairs, and she seated them at

a wooden table where they could look out the window toward the water.

"Yall drink red wine?" she asked.

"Yes," they replied together.

"Is the sky blue?" Paul added.

"It seems to be," Zoe said, as she opened a bottle to set on the table with three glasses. "But maybe it just seems that way." Then she set out a platter with barley crackers, a piece of hard cheese with a knife, and a pot of honey with a spoon in it. Finally she put down small plates and napkins, then sat down herself and poured the wine. "This is California Zinfandel," she said. "I only drink California wine." She took a sip, closed her eyes, and swallowed. She picked up a cracker and said, "I don't know if you've ever tried this, but put a little bit of cheese on the cracker, then some honey on the cheese. Of course, if you don't like it, then don't do it."

They tried it and Paul found it slightly odd, but perfectly fine at the same time.

"How do you like it with honey?" she asked.

"I do like it," he said. He took another bite, chewed some more, then added as he held his cracker in the air, "'Honey is not for the ass's mouth.'"

"My cousin does proverbs," Luke said.

"Delightful," said Zoe. "They add grace to a conversation." She turned toward Luke. "So you're visiting Charleston for a few days?"

"Yes, mostly trying to track down this letter that doesn't seem to exist."

"What sort of letter?"

Paul shook his head and said, "A letter from Catherine the Great."

"What!" Zoe looked shocked. "Seriously? Maybe we should look again. I want a letter from Catherine the Great to be discovered in my house." She stared open-mouthed, a disbelieving gape. "Now I'll join you in being sorry that it's the wrong desk. And why would there be a letter from Catherine the Great?"

"Apparently she wrote a letter to Henry Middleton, one of our ancestors."

"Henry Middleton? So your family and my family both have deep roots here in Charleston. Maybe your ancestors owned my ancestors. I'm Gullah, although you can't tell it from the way I talk now. My mother went off to New York to go to school, so I grew up partly outside the Gullah culture, even though I was born here."

"I've heard the name Gullah," Luke said. "But I don't really know what it is."

"The Gullah were the black people who lived out on the islands. They had their own culture and language even, based on English, although I think the language is dying out. I don't speak it. Have you seen the women around town in Charleston selling the sweetgrass baskets?"

"Like the baskets you have here?"

"Yes, I have a lot of sweetgrass baskets, from my relatives, actually. So you've seen the basket sellers?"

"Are they Gullah?"

"Yes, those are Gullah women. That type of basket is one of the crafts that came over from Africa. It's my heritage, but I don't know how to make the baskets."

"I suppose you could paint pictures of people making baskets," Paul said.

"I've done that, and I guess that's as close as I'll get."

They continued eating cheese and crackers and honey, they continued with the wine so that Zoe opened another bottle, and the breeze continued to come in the window with the smell of salt. Waves continued out on the water, the earth continued to race into the darkness, and bees continued home to the hive.

"How do you like living sort of isolated like this?" Luke asked Zoe.

"I love it," she said. "I don't know how people could live in town." She shook her head. "Really, I don't."

"I live in town," Paul said. "It's wonderful. I like the restaurants."

"I like good food, too," Zoe said. "But it really suits me out here. I'd even say it has a kind of dreamlike quality, being so surrounded all the time by the water and the sky and the light. I like dreams. Every morning I write my dreams down when I wake up. So I like living in a dream."

"But you're just using a figure of speech," Paul said. He poured himself another glass of wine.

"Why do you think?" she asked.

"I mean…to say that this is like living in a dream, that it's a kind of illusion."

"No, I mean it seriously," she said. "I didn't say it's *like* a dream." She bent her head slightly forward, as if she were going to look up from under her eyebrows. "I said I like living in a dream."

"Yeah, OK," Paul said. "But I mean—" He tapped his fingers on the table. He assumed she must be making some kind of joke about living in a dream.

"So you don't think dreams are real?" she asked. "I think they are. Or they're— no, no wait. I'm not being clear. Everything is the same, the dream world, this world. I don't mean to say that dreams are real. Maybe I meant just the opposite, that *nothing* is real, or rather, nothing is more real than anything else. It's all an illusion."

"Then what *is* real?" Paul said.

"We can't know that," she said. "But this is all just a dream, so why not live in a good dream, like this island."

Luke took another piece of cheese and looked at it. "Not real cheese," he said, holding it up.

"Not real wine," Paul said, lifting his glass.

"If nothing is real," Luke said, "then nothing matters."

"No, no, no," Zoe said. She held both hands up in front of her, with one finger raised on each hand. "Things do matter. Some things matter a lot, like love.

But the world we live in is just an illusion. Does the idea bother you? This table isn't really solid, this wine isn't really red. And you and I aren't any more real than they are. Ultimately we all just fade away, as if God woke up."

Four lines of poetry by Akhmatova repeatedly came back to Luke afterward, though later he wanted to forget them. *Everything is gone, both strength and love. In this harsh city the abandoned body no longer cares about the sun. I feel that my blood has grown completely cold.*

It was October, and Ray, the Cultural Affairs Officer, appeared in the doorway of Luke's office, looking pale. "Your wife has been in an accident," he said. There was a sudden feeling for Luke of unreality. As soon as he understood what was being said, Ray's voice started to sound far away, and Luke felt a sudden cold, cramped feeling in his stomach. *No no no* went through his head. Ray told him that Selia had been crossing the street and had been hit by a car. Why didn't Ray go on and tell him that she had been killed? Maybe he didn't know. Or maybe she was still alive when Ray found out.

By the time Luke got to the hospital, Selia was gone. That morning she had suggested they go out for pizza in the evening, she was reading the paper when he left, she looked up and said goodbye as he was going out the door. By four o'clock she wasn't in the world anymore. Without the help of friends, Luke would have lain down in the hospital and been done. Or maybe if he had been allowed to lie there long enough, stunned and living now in a different world, he would have gotten up eventually, to drag himself outside where everything, the street, Moscow, Russia, the planet Earth, had turned gray. But friends came, they took him home, they put their arms around him, and they caused him after two days to eat and drink. The days in Moscow then were turning into winter and growing shorter, but what did it matter to Luke, light or dark? All was dark. He went through that time not caring if he ate or bathed or spoke or fell to the ground forever. Other people arranged for Selia to be cremated.

Because they had been young and healthy and enjoying life, Luke and Selia had given little thought to what to do if they died. They weren't going to die, so it wasn't necessary to think about it. But when Luke had to, he took her ashes back to her home in North Carolina and buried them there. Selia's family had lived in the mountains of the western part of the state for generations. Luke flew from Moscow to New York, changed for a flight to Charlotte, then a final short flight to Asheville. Selia's brothers, John and Griffin, met him in Asheville, and they hugged without speaking. None of the three men knew how to express his own grief, and they didn't know how to help each other. Griffin, a strong man who worked as a carpenter, carried the casket with Selia's ashes, a box made of fake marble. Luke barely spoke during the hour drive from Asheville down to Sylva, through those mountains still filled with autumn leaves. In all the years Selia had been gone, her brothers had stayed in the mountains and made lives in the village where they grew up, and now they were taking their sister home.

The funeral service was in the same Methodist church where Luke and Selia had gotten married. In spite of his numbness and distraction of grief, Luke was surprised at how many people filled that small church. Spending most of his life with Selia in other countries, he almost came to think that the two of them composed each other's world, each other's universe even, with the occasional comet of a friend or family member flying through. It was almost as though Luke had thought, cut off overseas the way they were, that it was really only him who had loved Selia, as if he was all she had. In that little church in North Carolina, he saw friends who knew her from high school, teachers who had taught her, acquaintances of her family, cousins and aunts and uncles from around the mountains, all coming into that little church, dressed in dark colors, people with solemn faces, people Luke didn't know, coming up to hug him. He saw that many people had loved Selia, not just him. Without him, she would have had other people to turn to—she had a family and a community.

Standing there being hugged by strangers, Luke suddenly realized that it wasn't Selia who had no one else. It was him who had no one but her.

There was a short memorial service, with the preacher for the church speaking, and then Selia's brother John spoke. He talked about things they had done as children, talked about Selia's sense of humor, and at one point he even managed to laugh at something she had once done. He also talked about her ambition to get out and see the world. While he was talking, he stopped in the middle of a word and stood silent a moment, looking down, visibly swallowing, but then he went on to talk about how much Selia liked the life she and Luke had been able to live in other countries. Then he pulled out a gift Selia had given him, a little wooden Russian doll, the sort that people in America call nesting dolls, and he stood it on top of her small casket. Following the service, the small casket with Selia's ashes was going to be carried out by John and Griffin, as pall bearers. Before they went up to take the casket, Luke sat looking at it, looking at that Russian doll that John had placed on top. The ashes of Luke's wife were in that box, the woman he had held in his arms, whispered to, whose body he had caressed while making love, who he had walked down streets with, thrown snowballs at—all in that box. Suddenly the small shore of Luke's body could no longer contain that ocean of grief. He laid his head down on his arms on the back of the pew in front of him and began crying, trying to be silent, as he strangely felt ashamed in front of all those people. One of Selia's cousins put her arm around him, and he leaned over toward her because he needed to lean on someone.

The burial was immediately after the service, and the crowd of people went to the cemetery, where the casket was lowered into a small hole that had been dug earlier. The preacher said a few words, and Aliselia Rosemiller was back in the ground that she had come from.

After the service, Luke looked at the mountainsides that surrounded them, mountains still covered with the bright red and orange and yellow of autumn. The hills were beautiful, and those trees were the first colors Luke had noticed since the moment when he had been told that Selia was in an accident. Maybe he noticed the colors at that moment because his mind sought respite from the fatigue of grief. Perhaps it was because he had always preferred autumn over other seasons and was accustomed to noticing it. As he stood there, he had a sudden thought of wanting Selia to see the trees, and that thought clutched at his throat, so that it was hard to breathe for a minute. *But she does see them* he told himself. He was a religious person, and he believed he would see her again in the next world. Still, it was unbearable how much he missed her in this one.

In the heavy, warm air, music came drifting through the small yards where palm trees grew. Paul listened to the music, a melancholy tune. He couldn't understand the words, but it sounded sad, like a soft sadness was floating out into the air. What language was it? Spanish maybe? Could it be some form of Latin that had absorbed sadness over the centuries?

"Do you know this music?" he asked Luke. They sat out on the small balcony of Paul's apartment, drinking glasses of brandy.

Luke listened for a moment. "No, I don't think I've ever heard it. It sounds like Portuguese."

"Portuguese," Paul repeated. "It's interesting." He listened another minute, then asked, "Did you ever play an instrument?"

"Yeah, I played flute," Luke said.

"You did?" Paul turned around in his chair to face Luke. "You played a *flute*?"

"Now why are you so surprised? You asked me if I played anything, and I told you."

"I don't know." Paul settled back into his seat and swirled the brandy in his glass, held it up to sniff without drinking. He didn't speak for a moment, then said, "I guess I would have figured maybe guitar or trumpet or something."

Luke looked over at him. "I played that third one. Something. I played flute in high school."

"And where was that?"

"In Germany."

"You've lived an odd life." Paul tried to picture his cousin playing a flute. He couldn't do it.

"Huh," Luke said. "I tell you I played a flute, and you say I lived an odd life. There's nothing wrong with the flute."

"No," Paul said. "I like a flute. Jethro Tull…"

"James Galway."

"Whoever that is."

"Whoever that is," Luke repeated sarcastically. "Did you play anything?"

"No. I'm the complete opposite of every kind of talent," Paul said. He held one hand out before him and motioned with each statement. "I can't draw. I can't play anything. I can't speak a foreign language."

"But you can teach college," Luke said.

"Oh yeah. Monkeys could teach college. Maybe not math, monkeys are a little too excitable to teach math, but most subjects anyway. Speaking of which, I need to run by my office for a while in the morning, and then I want to go back out to the house Aunt Lindy gave me. I want to make a closer inspection if it really seems ready to move into."

"It looked like it."

"Yeah, it did, but I didn't look very closely at the electrical connections. I don't want any problems for Rachel."

"So you're going to—"

"I don't know, I'm just…" He didn't finish the

sentence. "I was thinking in the afternoon we could go start searching Aunt Lindy's house."

"Yeah, that damned desk," Luke said. "So what could have happened with that desk?"

"I don't know. The guy at the store checked his book. And he knows he bought it."

"Maybe that's a mistake too." Luke frowned and sighed.

"No, no, he bought it. He knew Aunt Lindy."

"How about this?" Luke said. "While you go to your office in the morning, I'll go back over to the store and double check with the guy. Maybe I can find something out."

"Yeah, if you want to," Paul said. "It won't hurt."

They sat silent for a couple of minutes, sipping their brandy and listening to the unknown music. Perhaps the woman singing was expressing her hopeless longing for the wretch who betrayed her. That happens a lot.

"I was thinking about what Zoe said this afternoon," Luke said finally. "It seems like mostly a metaphor."

"What?"

"That life is a dream."

Paul shook his head. "How can something be mostly a metaphor?"

"I mean not entirely true," Luke said.

"Something can be partly true," Paul agreed, "but

a metaphor is a figure of speech. Either you use it, or you don't."

"OK, whatever, but you know what I'm saying."

"But are you saying that life is partly a dream and partly not?"

"Maybe it depends on the point of view," Luke said. "Or on how you define 'dream'. If you mean it literally, like somebody's asleep and just imagining all of us, then I don't believe that."

"Maybe God's imagining us, like Zoe said."

"No, that's too simple. But to say everything's an illusion in the sense that it's mysterious and we don't know what's going on—" Luke breathed heavily— "that I'll agree with."

"I drink to dreaming," Paul said, and raised his brandy glass.

"I dreamed about Selia last night," Luke said.

Paul paused a couple of seconds, then said, "That must have been a hard dream to have." He frowned to think of it but didn't look over at Luke.

"I dream about her sometimes. When I wake up from those dreams, I'm sorry I woke up. It's almost like having her die again."

Paul found what Luke said so sad and depressing that he wasn't sure how to respond. He wanted to say something comforting to his cousin, but the things that came to mind sounded trivial and wrong, so he just sat quietly and felt awkward.

After a long silence, Luke spoke again. "I wonder if

a time comes when you stop missing somebody every single day. Can you suffer that feeling of loss every day for your whole life? I don't want that."

"I don't know," Paul replied. "Of people close to me, I've only had Mama die. And I don't guess that's anywhere near the same as a wife."

"I know what I ought to do," Luke said. "I mean, I know what the right thing is. I ought to get on with life, try to enjoy it. I'm trying to do that here."

"Yes." Again Paul wanted to say something comforting and felt stupid and a little guilty for not knowing what to say.

"But I miss her every day," Luke said. "I'm not in control of that, I just do. I'd stop it if I could."

They sat silently as the music below played.

"Are we better off not to get so close to someone?" Paul asked. Then he felt stupid for saying this. The conversation naturally made him think about Rachel, what it would be like to lose her. The thought that he could lose her gave him a cold chill.

Luke turned toward him, and Paul could see that Luke's eyes were shining, bright with tears. "No," Luke said. His voice sounded heavy and wet. "To never love somebody? That would be worse."

They sat a while more, until finally Luke said, "I'm kind of tired. I think I'll turn in." They both stood up and went into the apartment, but instead of going to his bedroom, Luke sat down on the couch. He sat still, staring ahead.

Paul looked at him, then asked, "Are you OK?"

"Yeah. Yeah, I'm OK. I think I might like to watch TV a little bit before I go to bed."

"Alright. Where did I leave the remote? The second it leaves my hand it's lost. You wouldn't believe…I found it in the refrigerator once." He began moving objects off a side table, and he lifted a small statuette of a woman praying with her hands together.

"That looks familiar," Luke said.

"You gave it to me," Paul replied.

"Oh. Selia bought it in Berlin."

Paul found the remote control for the TV and handed it to Luke, who turned on the TV and began moving through channels. Paul stood a moment more looking at him and thought that with Luke sitting there, it was hard to picture him being in all those places. It was hard to picture him in Russia.

The Witch in Moscow: Feeling Foolish

If you want to call a Russian witch an "enchantress", you might try the word "charodeika". Some language scholars have said that "charodeika" and the English word "charm" go back to a similar source, though we should acknowledge that this is strongly disputed by other linguists. In any case, a person may be enchanted by a charodeika in a variety of ways, as she may charm you with perfume, perhaps, or with the smell of peaches, or maybe with the swirled scent of wine.

SELIA WAS CHARMED by Russian churches, perhaps partly by the smell of incense and candles. Luke would sometimes go with her to visit churches, though it was never the same for him as it was for her. The last church they were in together before she died was the Spassky Cathedral in the Andronikov Monastery. This was the monastery of Andrei Rublev, the greatest icon painter of Russia, a painter so skilled that he became famous in an art form that was never signed, in which the artist was painting only for the glory of God. A week before Luke left Moscow for the last time, in December, he went back to the Andronikov Monastery, to think about when he was there with Selia, to think about her in a quiet spiritual place where they'd been together.

There was a foot of snow on the ground, and the day was very cold. The monastery no longer functioned as a religious institution, having been converted into the Rublev Museum, but the Spassky Cathedral had been turned back into an operating church, and it was the church that he was actually there for. He went through the gates of the monastery, crossed a snowy courtyard, and went into the church, grateful to get out of the bitter cold. The church was also cold, but warmer than outside. He stood inside holding his fur hat in his hands, looking at the icons painted on the walls and columns and remembering how studiously Selia had moved, walking slowly around the church as she stared at the painted walls. On this final return visit to the church, Luke saw candles burning here and there, flickering in the dim light of the cold space.

He stood looking at the painted wall of the iconostasis at the front, with paintings of Jesus and Mary and rows of saints, when his attention was caught by a woman who had come in with her daughter. The woman wore a brown scarf over her hair, tied under her chin. The girl held a fur hat but also had a scarf tied around her head. Luke guessed that the mother had put the scarf on her daughter as they came in. It wasn't clear how old the woman was, but she seemed to be about as old as Selia. Luke moved away from the iconostasis and walked around a column to watch them better. The girl was young, maybe eight, and her mother had bought a candle which she gave to the daughter to light and place in front of one of the icons. Then they both crossed themselves, with the girl watching her mother, imitating her, and afterward the mother closed her eyes and bowed her head for a minute to pray. When she did, Luke bowed his head and prayed along with her.

At last Luke felt he had calmed some of the spiritual hunger that had brought him there, and he left to trudge through the snow to the Ploshchad Ilyicha metro station. In the crowded metro, filled with rushing people, bright lights, and fast trains, he tried to hold on to some of the quiet tranquility from the church. For a while as he waited for a train and after he first got into the car, he turned over in his mind images of the icons painted in the church and images of the mother and child lighting a candle. In the noisy, bright train, however, he began to pay attention to some of the other passengers. He knew he was leaving Russia, and he wanted to remember.

An old man sat on the bench across from him. When Luke had been a student in Moscow, he had seen more old men like this, but since then many of them must have died. The man wore a dark coat and an old worn fur hat. He was obviously of the World War II generation, because he still followed a common Soviet practice of wearing all the medals he had been awarded during the war on his civilian coat. He sat there with a blank expression, with those small colored rectangles lined up in neat rows on his coat, reading a book that had been carefully wrapped in newspaper. Down at the end of the same bench were two other men, perhaps in their thirties, nicely dressed in new suits with white shirts and dark ties, talking softly together. One of the businessmen pulled out a cellphone, used it to check the time, and put it back in his pocket. To the right sat a woman in her fifties, or perhaps sixties, a short fat woman, wearing a print dress and a white scarf, with rubber boots on her feet. She was a homely woman, red-faced, and carrying three cloth bags that were jammed with whatever she had been buying or selling. The large dirty bags were so full they took up part of the aisle in an inconvenient way for other passengers.

When Luke was changing trains, he saw two men apparently in their twenties, laughing and talking, both dressed in black pants and boots. One wore a heavy denim jacket, and the other had on a brown leather coat. The one in leather had an unlit cigarette stuck in the corner of his mouth. Both of the men had their heads shaved and no hats. They also both had a symbol which Luke didn't recognize, tattooed on the back of their necks. As they were talking, another man passed, and the one in denim turned to his companion, narrowed his eyes, and muttered "kike".

Leaving the metro, Luke tried to fit the variety of people he had just seen into a pattern, wanting to find some meaning in this place where his wife had died. The woman in the church, the skinheads, the old man, they all moved about in Luke's thoughts, unable to sit together, in spite of his efforts to see any connections. He walked toward the underpass to Old Arbat Street, and he added the gypsy witch Bella to the confusion of people in a confusing country in his own confusing life. He hoped he would find Bella where he had seen her before. There was no reason to expect her in such cold weather, and in the middle of winter, but he hoped. He wasn't sure why he wanted to see her again, since both incidents with her before had left him with nothing but mystery, and wasn't life already tainted with more mystery than anyone needed? Even so, he wanted to see Bella one more time, to see what magic she might show him.

He walked down through the underpass, where a couple stood talking, and in the same spot, he found her squatted down, wearing a large green, fringed scarf tied over her hair. This time there was no cardboard spread out, and no icons, but standing up against the wall where the image of Gabriel had stood before, there was a rectangular object covered with a black cloth. Luke was glad to see her, but surprised to find her with nothing except this black-covered rectangle, which he assumed, from the size, was one of her icons. He stood without saying a word until she rose to her feet. She also said nothing, but instead slowly closed her eyes and slightly lowered her head, then raised one hand pointed toward him. He wasn't quite sure what she wanted, but seeing that her eyes remained closed, he closed his own. After a few seconds he thought *I feel foolish*, as nothing seemed to be happening, so he opened his eyes. When he did, Bella was looking at him, and still without speaking, she held her hand out and lowered it, closing her own eyes. He assumed again that she wanted him to close his eyes, and again he did so.

Now he stood quietly in the underpass, feeling himself breathe. Because there were no icons with Bella, he figured he was not going to see anything, and as he let go of that expectation, he felt unexpectedly relaxed. He waited what seemed like a long time, just standing and breathing, but he tried to be patient, and then he was astonished by the pungent, sweet scent of fresh flowers. He almost opened his eyes but kept them closed. He had not seen or smelled any flowers as he approached the spot where he stood, and in such a place, surrounded by snow, the smell now was a shock. As he breathed in the smell of flowers, he caught something more subtle, a smell of perfume, and then he noticed a slight scent of sweet chocolate. The longer he stood, the more clearly he could smell these pleasant things.

The second he opened his eyes, he smelled nothing. He looked around. No flowers, no chocolate bar, nothing to produce the smells. When he looked back at Bella, she nodded at him, then squatted down again and ceased to pay him any attention.

Paul and Luke sat in a restaurant on King Street, talking with their waitress, who wore a green scarf tied around her waist. "I don't eat eggs," the waitress said.

"That cuts out most of your menu," Paul told her.

"That's OK, the customers eat them," she replied.

"Well, I'll have the Eggs Southern." He closed his menu and looked at a painting on the wall.

"And what about you?" she asked Luke.

"This frittata looks pretty serious. I'll try that."

"You want to add smoked salmon or snow crab?" she asked.

"No, I think the other fifteen ingredients will be enough." He also closed his menu and handed it to her.

"Alright, I'll be right back with yalls juice." They sat at breakfast Thursday morning in The Bakers Café, near the antiques stores. A gospel song was playing.

"I've been noticing something around here," Luke said. "What are these metal plates you see on the sides of buildings all over town? Do you know what I'm talking about? Here and there you notice it up on the side of the building."

"Yeah," Paul replied, "those are the ends of long metal bolts that run through the building." He saw the disbelieving look on Luke's face. "No, seriously. After the earthquake in 1886 they ran those bolts through a lot of the buildings and then tightened them up to hold the buildings together."

"So all these buildings have been bolted back together?"

"A lot of them."

"I never thought of Charleston as having earthquakes," Luke said. Luke apparently had not yet realized that Mother Earth will hurl us around whenever and wherever she damn well pleases. The waitress came up carrying two glasses of orange juice, also courtesy of Mother Earth.

"It hasn't been a problem lately," Paul said, "and it's been over a hundred years, but it was a huge one then. I've read that the quake was felt hundreds of miles away."

"Well," Luke said. "That's pretty interesting." And so it was, what with the screaming and fires and widespread terror.

"Yeah." Paul drank his glass of orange juice. "We've got more history here in Charleston than we know what to do with. That's why we sell some of it to the tourists." He looked at Luke. "We'll sell you some."

"I've got enough of my own."

After breakfast, Paul walked back to his apartment for his car to drive to the college. It wasn't particularly far away, but Paul saw walking as a kind of punishment for foolishness, for having put yourself in a situation where you needed to walk. He drove to the campus, went to his office, and while he was there the phone rang.

"We followed the wrong desk," Luke said to him.

"Yeah, I noticed," Paul replied. "I was there when it happened. Did you talk to the dealer?"

"Yeah, I went back to the same store and talked to the owner again. You're not going to believe it."

"Test the limits of my imagination."

"The Hollingsworths bought two desks at the same time. The dealer swears they bought Aunt Lindy's desk."

Hope awoke, stretched, and sat up with a sly smile, but then Paul felt irritated. "So why didn't he tell us this to start with?"

"I thought so too," Luke said. "He just said we were asking about a particular desk, and he told us what happened to it."

"Yeah, good for him," Paul said. "So he says they've got the desk?"

"I guess they do, unless they've sold it to the king of England."

"They have a queen now."

"Yeah, her too."

"Alright." Paul tapped on the papers in front of him. "I'm about to go back out to the beach to look at the house. I'll be home in about two hours, but first I'll call the Hollingsworths again."

"I'll meet you at the apartment," Luke said. "I'm going to walk around and look at the town."

"Alright, I'll meet you for lunch. Walk down to the Battery. That's a nice walk."

Before Paul arrived at his new house, he passed three couples out walking and pushing baby carriages. Had people always been pushing baby carriages, or was he just noticing them now? He wondered whether Rachel wanted to have children. She was only in her mid-thirties, so it wasn't too late. What if she did? Did *he* want them? It was a completely scary idea and not something to be thinking about. Even as he didn't think about it, he saw her sitting at her kitchen table wearing a robe, drinking coffee, looking up at him as he walked into the room. Seeing him, she smiled, then blew on her coffee.

When he got to his house, he turned into the sandy drive, got out of the car, and looked again at the palmetto bushes, narrowing his eyes. Absolutely that spiky nonsense was getting cut down. Put in some azalea bushes, maybe. He went again into the shade under the house, and this time he stopped by each post, looking at it more carefully from bottom to top. It all seemed very solid and unaffected by decay.

A neighbor was coming down the stairs of the house next door, a woman in her forties with dark curly hair and wearing sunglasses with red frames.

The woman was a little overweight, and she wore a one-piece bathing suit with an open blouse over it. "Are you the new owner?" she asked.

"I am," Paul said. "How do you know about that? I just found out myself."

"Word gets around," she said, slightly shrugging and lifting one eyebrow. "Welcome to the neighborhood. Is it gonna be a summer place?"

"I don't know. I'm thinking about living here."

"Well, I went through the last hurricane with no problem. I'm Maryellen." She shook Paul's hand. "I moved down here five years ago from Ithaca, New York. Got tired of living in snow. I'll take hurricanes."

Paul went up the stairs to his own deck, pushing on the railing to test it, and felt satisfied. Inside the house he scowled again at the color of the walls, then began looking for electrical sockets and noticing where all light switches and overhead lights were located. In one of the rooms, he looked out the window and imagined standing in the room with Rachel, in their bedroom, watching storms come in from the ocean, with great walls of black clouds rolling in as he put his arms around her. Finally he went back out onto the deck and looked toward the calm sunny ocean, then took photographs looking out at the water. Standing there, feeling the breeze try to blow away the rising heat, still thinking about Rachel, he recalled standing in a store downtown with her picking out candles for the evening.

"What about this one?" he had asked, picking up a fat green candle five inches tall.

"No, I want the long thin kind," she had replied. "Taper candles."

"This would last longer."

"I don't care how long they last," she said. "I like the thin ones better. They're more graceful. Don't we want gracefulness?" She picked up a couple of eight-inch long tan candles. At dinner that evening she explained that she started to like candles from going to Catholic church services as a girl. At her church in Ohio, they had used a lot of candles.

Looking at the tan candles she was holding, Paul said, "OK, those are nice".

"Mmmmm, no. Brown isn't right. We want something with color. Graceful but pizzazzy." She put the candles down, then picked up another pair. "How about this blue green? They remind me of the water here."

If you stand at the very tip of Charleston, down at the Battery, you can see boats on the water and birds above the water, and somewhere out in the middle of that water is where the Civil War started. There stands Fort Sumter on its island, in all its defiant, apocalyptic glory. Charleston is almost like being in Europe, where the history is so heavy it has to be moved out of the way sometimes to be able to do things. Luke had also found that Russia was like that, history like a thick mud that would suck you down until you couldn't move.

From Charleston's Battery, he walked back up toward Market Street admiring the town. In that part of Charleston, on the peninsula between the rivers, everything appeared beautiful and well kept up. It was the area of town where Aunt Maryanne lived. Many houses in Charleston had a type of fake front door facing the street. Going through that door left a person still outside, standing on a long porch facing the bay, with the actual entrance to the house coming from the porch. Such porches had once been very popular, as a place to sit privately in the breeze before the invention of air conditioning. The houses near the Battery also had small yards, visible in some cases through closed gates, with manicured neat grass, flowers, shrubs, banana plants, and the usual palms. Luke loved the slightly tropical, slightly colonial feeling of the area.

The flower boxes at the windows especially appealed to him, with flowers in wild and reckless abandon, pushing one another in crowds out of those boxes. In some cases the town itself had planted flowers in baskets that hung from the palm trees along the sidewalks. Some of the large public buildings had a Greek appearance, as though temples had been plucked up from the Mediterranean and set down on the coast of the new world. Some of the houses down near the Battery were three stories tall, with wide porches on two or even three levels. Luke walked past the houses, looking up at the rows of porches, wondering who could have lived in such luxury? Of course, there are people in the world who live even now in much greater opulence. In Luke's experience, these were certainly not the most ostentatious displays of immoral wealth he had ever seen. Russian nobility had built preposterous palaces where you sometimes get the feeling they decided to simply splatter the walls with gold and toss jewels in afterward.

A couple of times while walking the Mediterranean streets of Charleston, Luke stopped into small art galleries to look at the paintings and pottery. He wondered whether Zoe Kirk's paintings were in one of the little yellow or blue galleries. She had said she sold things here in Charleston, but he didn't see anything that evoked her style until he came to the Trois Enfants Gallery. In a window he found two pictures of islands viewed from the water, looking like Zoe's paintings. He went in and inquired, and he felt happy to see that they were hers, to find something by an artist he knew. He stood for a while looking at her work, thinking about being out at her house, in her studio, remembering their conversation.

Eventually he wandered up the peninsula to Market Street, where a covered market stood in the middle of the street for several blocks. Parts of the market had been enclosed as individual businesses, such as a hat shop, but other sections had open spaces filled with the tables and stands of people selling a variety of goods, and Luke wandered in to escape the heat of the sun. The aisles between the tables were packed with tourists in shorts, T shirts, and baseball caps or capless visors. Old people with gray hair wandered the market, young couples carried babies in backpacks, and parents told their children they could spend $5 each. Very young children wanted to be on their own as long their parents stayed clearly in sight, and teenagers desperately did not want anyone to know they were with their parents. People were buying T shirts that said "Charleston" or "South Carolina" or misspelled banalities such as "Ya'll come back, now", they were looking through the recycled jewelry in large cases, and they were asking if the fancy children's clothing was machine washable.

Just as he had once done in Moscow in his games with Selia, Luke watched people. A fat middle-aged white man sat in a plastic chair. He wore a long heavy beard and a blue sailor's hat with gold braid, and he kept repeating, "Cheap and good" in a hoarse voice. In front of him was a table covered with knives, some tiny and some large enough to slice up an elephant. He took off his captain's hat to wipe away sweat and was completely bald underneath.

The next stand sold various spices, along with a remarkable display of hot sauces, more varieties than Luke had imagined could be created, or needed to be. Once you've burned out the lining of your mouth, what else is there? A Hispanic couple was working the spice booth, a dark man with black hair, wearing a white T-shirt, and a tiny, plain-looking woman in a blue dress, who took packages of dried peppers out of a box and put them on a shelf.

There were other tables of jewelry, stands with dolls, Civil War memorabilia, and a table with batik cotton dresses. Selia had owned a couple of similar dresses when they were first married. A thin girl with hair dyed partly blonde and partly green was selling the dresses. She stood looking off into the distance, an expression of incredible boredom on her face, and it seemed to Luke that she clearly didn't care whether anyone bought anything, or whether they all just went to Hell. The girl had a pale complexion, and she wore three or four rings in each ear, with a ring above one eyebrow and a small stud sticking through the middle of her lower lip.

The third lesson in being here

WHEN I LEFT that covered market building, the intensity of the sunlight nearly knocked me down. It was also hot on the street, and I decided that I needed some ice cream. At a shop nearby I got a chocolate cone, which was perfect, because it was ice cream, and because it was chocolate. I was surprised how fast it started to melt in that awful heat, and I began licking faster. I walked along looking for some shade to finish my cone, which I found at the entrance of a restaurant with a covered canopy. A pot stood nearby with some kind of vinelike plant growing up a trellis, and the plant was covered with pink and rose-colored flowers. The flowers had a wonderful smell, and when my cone was almost gone, I closed my eyes and took a deeper breath. With my eyes still closed, I smelled a third scent, the perfume from a woman walking by.

This time, I almost wasn't surprised. Almost. Standing there with my eyes closed, enjoying those smells of chocolate ice cream, of flowers, of perfume, I realized this was the final thing I had experienced with Bella in Moscow, on that snowy afternoon, the last time I saw her. She had let me smell this combination of smells, in that cold Moscow underpass. The thing I was looking for.

Opening his eyes, Luke saw a young black woman across the street, surrounded by baskets, sitting on the sidewalk just outside the entrance to the covered market. She was looking at him and continued to look even when she caught his eye. The baskets around her were the kind that Zoe Kirk had all over her house, and although it seemed a little silly to think so, Luke wondered if the woman could be one of Zoe's relatives. The woman had been weaving baskets as she sat there, taking bits of dried materials and twisting them in and out, but she had stopped weaving to focus on him.

He walked across the street to her but wasn't quite sure what to say, so to break the awkward silence, he asked, "Are these Gullah baskets?"

"Some people call 'em dat," she said. Now she looked down and began weaving again. "We call 'em sweetgrass baskets."

"Oh, sweetgrass," he said. "I heard that." Then he explained, "I'm not from around here."

"You a tourist," she said.

"Yes, I'm visiting my cousin." He paused a second, then said, "I'm Luke."

"How you do, Luke?" She nodded, but her hands

continued to weave the grasses in and out. "I'm Belle."

He was still wondering whether these were the baskets Zoe had talked about, so he asked, "But these baskets are from the Gullah culture?"

"Dat's right. I learn it off me nana. She teach me dem ol' ways." Listening to her talk, Luke figured the woman's speech must be from the Gullah dialect that Zoe had talked about.

"These are beautiful baskets," he said. He had truly never seen anything like them, made of coils of grass, the way a pot might be made of coils of clay, with a mix of light and dark grass and with pine needles to add more color and texture. The shape of the baskets was the thing that most appealed to him, as many of the handles looped around like twisting snakes or like rivers that flow apart then back together, like meandering paths through the sand dunes or streaks of clouds in the late evening sky.

Belle looked up at him while he was studying the baskets and said, "You be lookin' fo' sometin'."

"I'm not sure," he said. "I hadn't really thought about buying a basket. But I might."

"No," she said. "I ain' talkin' 'bout de baskets. You be lookin' fo' sometin' else."

"Looking for what?" he asked. "What do you mean I'm looking for something?"

"You lookin' fo' sometin' inside yose'f. Study yo' head, what you be lookin' fo'."

He only felt confused by the conversation. "Study my head?"

She twisted the grass and wove it in and out. Then he noticed that the basket she was working on, the weaving of dried, dead plants, had a live blade of grass growing up from the side of the basket. As he watched, the blade grew taller, growing green from the dead grasses of the basket. Several others sprang up around the edge of the basket, green shoots pushing up. "You lookin' fo' sometin' you missin'. Look inside yo' head. What you be missin'?"

It was astounding to find himself in a world where dead grasses could come to life, but at that moment, everything he knew about his life told him he should be standing right there, talking to this woman. He considered her question. What was he missing? What did she mean by that? He knew he was missing peace of mind. He was missing Selia. But it felt too personal to say that, and instead he said, "I'm missing a reason to go to so much trouble."

"Trouble 'bout what?" As Belle was talking, the basket she was holding grew into a full armload of living green grasses, weaving and twisting about as they grew. She was pushing the tall grasses apart to look at him.

"To go to so much trouble about what we do," he said. "About life. The same thing everybody thinks about, isn't it? It doesn't make sense."

"You want life to mek sense? Do you?" She was

looking at him intently, with those tall grasses around her.

"It's what everybody wants, isn't it?" he said. She surely could not think it was OK for life to be so senseless.

"Me and you got a differ on dat," she said. "Some people done figure out dey don' need dat."

"Don't need what? To know what life is about?"

"Dat's right. If life mek sense all de time, it lose de beauty of livin'. Why you want to live a life wid no mystery? Life widout mystery ain' no good life."

"OK, mystery," he said. He closed his eyes for a second, then opened them. "Maybe mystery is OK. But why are we *here*? Why get out of bed every morning?" Now every basket sitting on the ground around Belle burst into life. The green shoots grew thicker and taller, flourishing up around them.

"I don' know why *you* get out of bed," she said. "I hardly can say. I get out of bed to feed me cats and walk to de beach. I done be up early, befo' day clean, watch de sun. Den I say 'T'ank God fo' life and good healt'." The street and the market were gone, hidden by the tall grass, as though Luke and Belle were deep in a field near the shore. While Belle was speaking, a rabbit stuck its nose out of the thicket, then ducked back in.

What kind of reason was she giving him for getting out of bed? "I don't have cats," he said. "And I don't live near a beach."

"But you got sometin', and you live someplace. You got yo' life."

"It can't be that simple," he said. "If it is, why am I so confused?"

"I hardly can say why you confused," she replied. "But I tell what I t'ink is dis. Life be simple and be not simple, at de same time. Dat's why I t'ink we cain't understan' it, cause it don' make sense dat it be two different t'ings like dat. And me personal, I don' try to understan'. Life be all dat stuff God put in de worl', too much fo' my head. But sometime in de evenin' de moon done rise, and I smell de marsh, and den life seem simple."

"Paying attention to good things," I said.

"Whatever you like. But you wanna get rid of all de mystery, you never gon' be happy. Dash away dat idea, Luke. Dey's too much mystery in life, you never gon' get rid of it all. Jus' be in it. Dat's it. Jus' be in it." She moved to continue work on the basket, and suddenly all the tall grass was gone. They were on the street again, tourists moving past, going in and out of the covered market.

"I think I'd like to buy this basket right here," he said, and picked one up.

"Dat one cost t'irty-five dollars," she said.

"Oh," Paul said when Luke entered. Luke walked over to the table and set a basket down. "You bought a Gullah basket." Paul picked it up by one of the curving handles. "I love the way they do these. How was your walk?"

Luke reached out and ran his hand over the basket that had alternating light and dark bands. "OK. Good. It gave me a chance to do some thinking."

Paul set the basket back on the table. "You must've gone through the market area."

"That's where I bought it."

Paul turned to his cousin. "I called the Hollingsworths, and they really do have it. I talked to the wife and described the desk. She says it's on the boat, swears it's true this time. She seemed pretty apologetic and said if we want to come out around three o'clock, they're going to take the boat out with some people, and we can go with them. We can go ride on their house boat."

"Yeah," Luke said. "I think we'll find a letter from George Washington before we find one from Catherine the Great. But the boat ride sounds fun."

"It does sound fun, so let's do it. I want to write Rachel. Do you need lunch?"

"I'm fine. Take your time."

"I probably would anyway."

I took some pictures at the house, Paul wrote to Rachel. *I'll send them to you.* When he had finished writing, he went out to the balcony and saw that Luke had carried the new basket outside and put it underneath the pot with the violet. Seeing the plant reminded Paul that he really needed to water it. It looked pretty sad.

Luke understood Paul's love of Charleston. He wished Selia could enjoy the things he had enjoyed in the area with Paul. She would have loved exploring and experiencing new things, seeing the shops and architecture, going out to the island to see Zoe, and Luke knew for sure Selia would have been fascinated by the different plants and flowers around the town. Whenever Selia saw a plant she liked, she would examine it, look at the flowers, look at the leaves, and name the plants it reminded her of. Luke had always simply thought she was having fun, engaging in a casual hobby, but in the few days he had been in Charleston, he had begun to think that her interest was more than entertainment. It had added something to her life that he never understood.

As long as he knew Selia, she had an interest in plants. So many of his memories brought her back with a watering can, or plucking leaves, or just admiring something in every season of the year. He could see her with her hair tied back, picking flowers, and sometimes she would come up to him with a piece of some plant, and she'd shove it suddenly under his nose and say, "Smell this!" In the summer, she would put pots out on the porch or the window sill or on tables or shelves in the house, and in the small bit of yard they had in Virginia, she planted it full, as temporary as they were. In a public park in Berlin during the fall, when they had stopped in front of some huge bed of dark yellow flowers, she had said, "My God, like little suns."

"What kind of flower are they?" Luke had asked.

"I don't know," she said, sort of whispered it, continuing to stare at the flowers as if he wasn't there. "I don't know. How fantastic."

Summer, fall, spring, there was always so much for her. One spring while they were stationed in Beijing, a friend from the French embassy wanted to take them to meet a Chinese couple he knew on the outskirts of the city, where they had a small house. Their Chinese hosts led them through the house, which was rather modest, and when they came out into the garden, the man who had created the garden stood back slightly, smiling and waiting for them to admire what he had done. He was surely satisfied to see Selia exclaim with happiness and practically run forward into the garden.

"Can we look around?" she asked, turning back around.

"I'm very happy to show you," the man said, and the two of them walked over to a bed of irises that was in bloom.

Luke's friend and the Chinese woman sat down at the table, and Luke sat with them.

"Shall I pour us wine?" the friend asked.

The Chinese woman also spoke some English.

"Yes, please," she said. "For me. Your wife like flowers," she said to Luke.

"She loves all plants," he replied.

"Very good her. Flowers are good to spirit."

Most of the places Luke and Selia lived, plants could only be grown in pots in the house. The last couple of years they were together, she was cultivating violets, a type of flower she'd never done before, but she started buying them in Moscow. They had five pots of violets sitting on window sills, plants she kept blooming most of the time.

Luke came in once, and Selia was standing by a row of violets, bending over them. "How you doing?" she was saying. "Are you making more little flowers?" Then she turned around and saw him and looked embarrassed. After she died, Luke had to decide what to do with the plants. He couldn't take them all back to America, even if he had wanted to. Throw them away? That was inconceivable, obviously. When their friend Louis found out that he needed a place for the plants, Louis said he would take them all. Luke had had no idea Louis was interested in plants and told him that.

"There's so much you don't know about me," Louis said. "You mostly think I'm a gay man who drives a bus for a living. I've had flowers in flower shows."

"Did you ever talk about flowers with Selia?"

"Of course."

"Why did she love plants so much?" Luke asked.

"She never told you?" Louis responded.

"I don't know," Luke said. "Why do you think she loved them?"

"Because they're mysterious," he said. "She loved the mystery."

"Here's another article on those balloon people," Luke said. He was looking at a newspaper as he and Paul drove back out to see the Hollingsworths. "The balloon came down near the city of Bilaspur."

"Where is that?" Paul asked.

"I don't know. In India. It says there was a hole in the balloon and they came down next to a lake. They still had pictures of doves, so they gave the rest of them to a local school."

"Does that make sense to you? I mean flying around in a balloon, throwing out pictures of doves? What the hell was that about?"

Luke lowered the paper and stared out the window. "I don't know." He paused, then repeated, "I don't know." He looked over at Paul. "Maybe they just like balloons."

"That I understand. But what's with the dove thing? And why India?"

"Maybe it's just a beautiful country." Luke lifted the paper again and scanned the articles.

They were driving out of Charleston, up onto the bridge into Mount Pleasant, over the Cooper River.

Luke stopped reading to look at the view, then went back to the newspaper. "There's something here about a study that Americans are getting fatter."

"Yeah, why don't you read me that?" Paul said. He looked down at his belly. "That should make me feel good."

"You're not fat."

"I'm not skinny."

Luke was quiet while he read a bit more, then said, "This just seems to say that people are sitting on their fat butts and eating potato chips."

"And what do they say is wrong with that?" Paul asked.

"You know..." Luke laid the paper down again. "One thing you really notice a difference between here and Russia is how many more fat people you see in the United States. Most Americans don't get enough exercise."

Paul nodded slowly yes. "I know I don't get enough. I hate exercising."

"OK," Luke said, looking again at the paper. "So we move on to happier topics. Here's a company that wants to arrange for people to take vacations in space. They're actually taking deposits."

"Sure," Paul said. "But will the food be good."

"Wait a minute," Luke said, suddenly looking up and staring at Paul. "Aren't you supposed to have glasses on when you drive?"

"You know I forget them. They help me see in the

distance, but I can get by." He shrugged. He looked out at the road and didn't see a problem.

"Maybe I should drive?"

"No, I'm OK. I was driving without glasses until a couple of weeks ago."

"And you needed glasses, which is why you went and got some. Can you read the signs?" Luke turned back toward the windshield.

Paul took his right hand from the wheel and held it out toward Luke, spreading his fingers. "I'm alright. We're safe. Read me about the vacations in space."

Luke looked at Paul uncertainly. "OK…" He looked back down at the paper. "It says the company is taking deposits. It seems a little early to be taking deposits."

"I can see it someday," Paul said. "Where the men first landed on the moon, they're going to build a building over it, maybe a dome thing like everybody imagines, and then there'll be walkways so nobody walks on the original dust and messes up the footprints. Then they'll pressurize it, fill it with air, and groups of tourists will be walking along, looking down and saying 'so that's where the first man walked'. And some bored kid in the back, like one of my students, won't have the slightest interest."

"Yes," Luke said, smiling and looking at his cousin. "And then they'll walk out to the gift shop to buy T shirts that say 'I followed the footsteps'. And there'll be postcards and plastic NASA memorabilia and little holograms showing the first ship just as it lands on the moon. And there'll be kids whining at their mothers to buy it for them."

"And then," Paul said, "they'll leave the gift shop and go out into the mall that it's part of. And there'll be a Nike store where they can buy Lunar Strides, the latest shoe, and they'll go next door to eat at McDonalds, which'll be decorated with old photographs of astronauts."

"Makes you look forward to the future, doesn't it?" Luke said.

"It's just going to be another place where human beings live," Paul said. "I guess if it makes people happy."

"I don't think it does," Luke replied. "Constantly moving around doesn't make anyone happy. We move around because we're like amoebas pushing out pseudopods, filling some biological urge."

"Still OK by me," Paul said. "If people want to move around for no reason, let 'em do it." He paused, then said, "This search for the letter is seeming as crazy as flying across India in a balloon. I wonder if there really is a letter. Oh, what the hell." He blew out a loud breath. "Well, I know there was one. Aunt Maryanne and Aunt Lindy both said so."

"You really think you need that letter to write your book?" Luke asked.

"Well, no, I guess I don't. I started the book before I knew about the letter. But damn, what if I had a letter like that? I really want to get tenure, you know?" He glanced over at Luke. "I want to stay here. I like it here."

"Hey," Luke said, "You're going to do the book anyway. You'll finish it, and if a book will get you tenure, then you should get it."

"From your lips to God's ears."

Shortly they were headed down the street toward the Hollingsworth's. And there was the three-story house with white railing and arches on the ground floor, with the palm trees to the sides. This time there were cars in the driveway and parked in the street nearby.

Carlee Hollingsworth opened the door when they knocked. "Hello!" she said. "I'm glad yall came right out. We're about to take the boat out, and we were waiting for you. Come on in." They went into the house, where the only other person besides Carlee was a tall, thin black woman wearing a black dress. The woman was taking food off a table. "I'm so sorry about this mixup over the desk," Carlee said.

"It's been an adventure," Paul replied.

"I do have that desk you described on the phone. I'm so sorry I didn't show it to you last time you were here. Guy told me yall were looking for the desk that had been by the piano, and that's the one we gave to Zoe. I should have thought to mention the other one. And of course, Guy didn't have a clue that there was another desk."

"Maybe it's a twisted kind of luck," Paul said. "It gave us a chance to go boating and meet Zoe."

"And then she didn't have the one yall were looking for."

"It was nice meeting her, though," Luke said. "It was worth it for that."

"Oh, that's good," Carlee said. "She's also coming."

"Zoe's coming, too?" Luke asked.

"Yes, she's on her way."

Paul and Luke glanced at one another.

"And she said some nice things about yall, by the way," Carlee added. "Still, I'm sorry for the inconvenience, but I can show you the desk now. I even waited to let yall be the ones to look for your letter. But let's go down. Everybody else is already out on the boat. We can go through here." Paul looked around the living room, which had Persian carpets on hardwood floors, and antique furniture throughout the room.

"Yall got a beautiful place," he said. Paul knew that a college professor was lucky to even be allowed to walk through a house like this. Certainly never going to live in one.

"Thank you," she said. "We've worked hard to fix it up." She led them out onto the second-story deck, and down the stairs. The boat was sitting at the dock as before, but now they saw people standing on the boat, and there was music playing.

They crossed the yard and stepped onto the boat.

The music was louder, and Paul smiled hearing the Beatles song Good Day Sunshine.

Guy Hollingsworth opened the door onto the deck of the boat and came out. "Glad yall are here!" he boomed. "Sorry about the confusion. But it's a chance to join the party."

"Thanks for inviting us," Paul said.

"Yes, thanks," Luke added.

"We're glad to have you. And I guess yall want to see that desk, which I'm sorry, I didn't um…have any idea about. I just don't always know what's going on in my own house. Or houseboat." He laughed very loud. "Carlee thinks I'm a plant and doesn't tell me anything."

"Honey, you are a plant," she said. She turned to Luke and Paul. "Come inside and get yourselves a drink, and you can meet some other folks." She went on into the large enclosed area of the houseboat.

"Yes, let's get yall a drink and then we'll look at that desk," Guy said.

"A drink sounds good," Paul said.

Luke nodded. "A basic truth of life."

"That's right," Guy said. "It's a boat party, you can't beat it. And later we'll get the grill going. Yall like hamburgers? Hotdogs? Steak? Or maybe you're vegetarians. I think we've um…got something here for vegetarians. It's something I respect, but I could never do it. My sister was vegetarian for a while, but my Lord, I need real food."

"No, no vegetarians here," Paul said.

"Good. Good. Come on in."

Guy led them through the door into the air conditioned boat, a refuge from the heavy humid air outside. Good Day Sunshine was still playing, and in the middle of the room a little girl, around four years old, was dancing. Other people stood or sat round the room, watching the little girl in the middle, dancing enthusiastically. She moved her arms and shook her shoulders and didn't seem to care about anything.

"My granddaughter, Michelle," Guy said. "She loves the Beatles."

"As well she should," Luke said. "If a child is properly raised."

"So what would yall like to drink?" Guy asked. He turned to Luke with an expectant look.

"I'll have a beer," Luke said.

"Make that two beers," Paul said, holding up two fingers.

"OK, two beers for him," Guy said to Paul, pointing his thumb at Luke. "But what'll you have?"

Paul laughed. "I'll start with one and see how it goes."

While Guy was getting the beers, Paul glanced around the room, looking for Zoe, but didn't see her. He noticed a man sitting in a chair watching the girl dance. He was a white man, very fat, with a short beard and short curly hair. The fat man was wearing a bright Hawaiian shirt with bold flowers on it, and in spite of the air conditioning he was sweating, but he had a contented look on his face, and he nodded to the music. Standing beside the fat bearded man was a thin man with no beard. He was an elderly black man, but though he was old, he had a generally smooth face. His narrow eyebrows added to his somewhat elegant appearance. The elegance was also derived from his smooth, unwrinkled pants and shirt, black even in such weather, with the shirt buttoned right up to the top. The man also wore a black cone-shaped hat, woven of straw, with a very wide brim. Decorating the hat were leather patterns that made Paul think of African art. Perhaps most striking to Paul was a very ugly white man standing nearby, with a wide nose, fat lips that drew back to reveal crooked teeth, high cheek bones, and eyes that seemed sunken into his face. He had a somewhat dark complexion and was not very old, but then again, it was hard to tell. He was dressed in white shorts and shirt, as if he was going to play tennis, but what Paul found compelling about his appearance was how sheer damn ugly he was. Paul didn't want to stare at him, as anyone knows that staring is rude, and he felt sympathy for the man…but still. God almighty.

Guy came back and handed both Paul and Luke a beer. A young blond-haired woman came up to Guy and looked at the girl dancing. "Michelle's a firecracker, isn't she?" the woman said.

"She is," Guy said. "That's how kids should be." He turned to Paul and Luke. "Let me introduce yall to my daughter-in-law, Kelly. Unfortunately our son Mitch is out of the state right now, so he couldn't be here." Kelly had long straight blond hair, a high forehead, and a bright smile.

"How yall doing?" she said, and shook their hands. When she smiled, she looked very pretty.

"You folks'll have to excuse me," Guy said, "but I've got to check on some things for the party." He walked across the room to the captain's chair and console at the front and sat down to look at the controls.

"Is she your daughter?" Paul asked Kelly, indicating the little girl. He enjoyed watching the girl dance, and now a song by the Kinks had come on, so she was bouncing about to that. Such uninhibited happiness, the natural state of a person who is dancing from the heart.

"My little dancing machine," Kelly said.

Carlee came up to them at that moment. "Oh, you've met Kelly. Isn't she charming?" Carlee shone with a huge smile.

"Carlee." Kelly shrugged her shoulders and turned her head slightly to one side. "Don't embarrass me."

"But you are charming, dear. I tell that to everyone."

"I know." Kelly rolled her eyes slightly, then said, "I'm going to get Michelle a snack."

Carlee turned back to Paul. "Do you want to go see the desk before we get started?"

"No," he said. "I'll wait."

Luke turned and stared at him. "You'll wait? Why do you want to wait?"

"Do you really think we're going to find that letter?" Paul asked his cousin. "Let's let it be possible for a little longer. If it's on the boat it's not going anywhere."

Luke blinked a few times, then said, "OK."

Paul nodded. "Let's finish our beers first."

"In that case," Carlee said. "I'd like to introduce you to some people, if you don't mind."

"Sure."

She daintily led them over to the elegant black man. "Austin, these are two new guests, Luke and Paul. Like the saints." Paul slightly grimaced when she said this.

The man in the cone-shaped hat shook their hands. "How do you do?" he said. "It's nice to meet you."

"Austin is a literature professor," Carlee said.

"Yeah?" Paul exclaimed. "I'm a professor too, at the College of Charleston. Where do you teach?"

"At the University of Pennsylvania, in Philadelphia. I'm just down here for the summer. What do you teach at the College of Charleston?"

"History, with a concentration in Russian history. What do you teach?"

"English literature," the man said, "with a specialty in mysteries."

"Mysteries?" Luke asked. "I didn't know English professors specialized in something like mysteries."

"Not many do. But a lot of people read mysteries."

Carlee now pulled them away and across the room. "And you have to meet Nick," she said. She led them up to the ugly man dressed in white.

"Nick," she said. "Here's two gentlemen I want you to meet." The man smiled broadly at them and nodded in a pleasant way.

"This is Luke and Paul," Carlee said.

"How are you?" Paul said and shook Nick's hand.

"Nice to meet you," Luke said.

"Nick is an architect," Carlee said, "and he's been working on the most fascinating project. Don't you think so, Nick? He's doing a hotel in outer space."

Paul and Luke both perked up noticeably. "A hotel in space?" Paul said. "We were just talking about that."

"Really?" Nick said. "It's not a subject that comes up for most people."

"You've actually designed a hotel in space?" Paul asked.

"That sounds a little more definite perhaps than it really is. But I am working on what you could call a hotel, to be attached to the space station. There's a lot of science involved here, since I have to supply things hotels don't usually think about, like air. But I have to put some luxuries in there that the astronauts don't get, since people are going to pay to go there."

"Oh, my God, I don't understand that," Carlee said. "I hate to fly. Rockets, airplanes, even a balloon sounds bad. Like those two people who were flying in a balloon across India. Did you hear about that?"

"Actually I know them," Nick said. The cousins both looked astonished at Nick.

"You *know* them?" Paul asked.

"It's a couple from Spain, and the husband is an engineer I've worked with."

"How strange is this that you know them? And why are they doing that?"

"Fernán has always loved balloons, and he was always talking about some big balloon project. They're doing it for fun."

"But aren't they throwing out pictures or something?"

"Yeah, pictures of doves from Picasso."

"Why?"

"Lupina's an artist. That's his wife. She's done performance art in Valencia. I've never understood it, but anyway, the pictures were her idea. She was born in the same town as Picasso."

Carlee said, "You know doves are— Oh, there's Zoe." They all turned to see Zoe Kirk stepping through the door into the large cabin of the houseboat. She was wearing a forest green dress and a strand of deep yellow beads, a color that set off her dark brown complexion. She looked elegant and pretty coming in the door. "Zoe," Carlee called.

Zoe turned toward them, and a bright smile filled her face. She walked over and hugged Carlee, then turned to Paul and Luke. "What a nice surprise to see yall again," she said. "Carlee didn't tell me you were coming." She looked over at Carlee, then back at Luke. "I'm glad to see you."

"We didn't really know it either," Luke said to her. "We keep crashing in on the Hollingsworths. But this is lucky."

"Oh no," Carlee said. "You're not crashing in. I'm glad it worked out this way. And maybe you'll find the letter."

"Oh, your letter from Catherine the Great!" Zoe exclaimed. "I've been thinking about that letter."

"If you'll excuse me," Carlee said. "Zoe was the last guest, so I'll tell Guy to get underway."

"It really is a pleasure to see you again," Zoe said, facing Luke.

"Can I get you something to drink?" he asked.

"You know I like red wine," she replied. He smiled in turn and went to find her a glass.

"So you think the letter might be here?" she asked Paul.

"No, not really," he answered. "But Carlee swears she really does have our aunt's desk on this boat, so we'll look." They could feel the boat begin to move, and they turned to look through the glass walls at the dock and house receding. Luke returned with a glass of wine for Zoe.

"If you do find it, what do you hope it says?" she asked Paul.

"Hope? Hmm. I hope it says 'Congratulations on your persistence." He laughed. "I hope it says *molodyets*. That's Russian for 'good job'. Isn't it?" He looked over at Luke.

"Yep," Luke said.

"Well, I hope it does, too," Zoe added. She also laughed, openly and happily. "Good job."

"Oh!" Luke said. "Oh, hey, I saw some of your paintings at a gallery in town."

"Yes, I sell at Trois Enfants."

"Yeah, that was— actually, I don't remember the name of the place, but I saw they were in your style, so I went in and looked, and your signature was on them. I was glad to find them. I like your work."

"Thank you. I do like some of the things I gave them."

"A child of the sky and sea," Luke said.

"Yeah, I guess."

"That's what you said," Luke told her.

"Oh you—" She laughed. "You remember that?"

Carlee returned to them to say, "OK, we're underway. Let me know when you want to look at the desk."

"I guess let's go ahead," Paul said.

"May I go along?" Zoe asked.

"Sure," Paul said.

"It's upstairs," Carlee said. "Part of the upper deck is enclosed as another room. I put the desk up there. Why don't we go outside and go up the stairs there?"

The air was hotter outside, but there was a slight breeze from the movement of the boat. They walked up a set of stairs leading to an upper deck, where several people were standing enjoying the view, the breeze, the sun. The water was bright from the sunlight; other boats went by them in both directions, some with sails and some with motors. Paul looked happily out at the palms on the shore. God, Charleston was a great place to live. For a couple of seconds he admired the view, smiling, then turned with Carlee, Luke, and Zoe.

Carlee crossed the deck, with Paul and Luke behind her, and opened the door to a small upper cabin. They stepped inside and saw a desk pushed against one wall. It was made of dark wood, with one long drawer in front, with three side drawers down each side, and with handles of dull brass.

"That's it," Paul said. "That was Aunt Lindy's desk. Damn it, there it is."

Above Luke's desk at his apartment in Washington was a copy of the most well-known Russian icon, the Virgin of Vladimir. It shows Mary holding the baby Jesus and was named after the town of Vladimir, where it was kept for a while. When Luke looked at the icon, he sometimes thought about religion, and he sometimes thought about Russia, but always he thought about Selia. She had bought the copy of the icon above his desk, and she hung it in their apartment in Moscow. Perhaps the picture also reminded Luke of Selia because he saw the virgin in the picture as having sad eyes, which evoked his own sadness. Even moreso, the icon made him think of his wife because she loved icons so much.

When Luke and Selia first met, as students in Washington, he was once at her apartment where they were looking at a book on Russian culture, with pictures of icons at the beginning of the book. Selia showed him one and asked, "What does it look like to you?"

"It looks like people at a funeral," he had said. The icon was called Deposition of Christ. "I guess this must be Jesus wrapped up on top of the casket."

"Do you like it?" she asked.

It didn't much matter to Luke whether he liked it. It was an old icon, it was from Russia, and therefore it was interesting because of that. Why did he need to like it? In any case, it didn't seem to him like something he could like. It was too odd, too alien.

"Yeah," he had said. "I guess I like it." He probably thought he was giving the right answer with his slightly considered response.

"Why do you like it?" she asked. "What do you like about it?" Now that he was called on for an honestly thoughtful answer, he had to admit that he didn't actually *like* it in terms of positive appreciation.

Selia, as it turned out, did not like it at all. "Look how flat it is," she had said. "There's no depth. Everything is just right on top in two dimensions. And it's so unrealistic, with these figures in the middle of nowhere and those weird choppy mountains." She looked at a few more icons in the same book and didn't care for any of them.

When they finally moved to Russia, Selia had encountered the icons the same way Luke did, mostly in museums or in a church, looking at them from an interest in Russian culture in general, but with no particular appreciation for these religious paintings. Luke and Selia would go to the Tretyakov Museum and see the famous ones, Rublev's Trinity or the Virgin of Vladimir, they would look at a few others, and then they would move on to the nineteenth century paintings that really pleased them. Selia was always a good observer, however, and she began to take a closer look at the icons.

When Luke thought of it later, he thought he knew when it started. They were walking through the Tretyakov, in the icon section, and they saw a woman who wasn't very old, possibly forty, who stood praying in front of the Virgin of Vladimir icon. To Luke and Selia, the image was just a picture in a museum, but to this woman, it was a living religious object, and she stood there repeatedly crossing herself, moving her lips as she prayed softly. Selia pointed the woman out to Luke, and then they went on to another room. By coincidence, as they approached another icon, a young man in his twenties dropped to his knees while staring up at it. The icons in this museum had been put there during the Soviet period, as if they were only pictures, and now that God had mercifully removed the Soviet Union, people were still treating the icons as religious symbols. Selia must have been particularly struck by these two incidents coming together. On the way home, she kept talking about what icons must mean to the Russians. She also discovered that her North Carolina upbringing in a Methodist church partly connected her with this exotic, distant artform, since some of the stories told in the icons were Bible stories she had grown up with. Things she didn't know, such as the lives of saints, she began to learn.

The more Selia looked at the icons, the more she saw the differences in them. She would tell Luke, "This one is all painted with earth colors, red and brown and yellow," then later she would compare it to one in a book: "This one is cooler, with a lot of blue in it." Or she would buy an icon and then want to explain its composition to him. "Some icons just have one or two figures and nothing else, like portraits, but others are packed with details, like this one. Look at the hills and these buildings in the background." As Selia's interest increased, she moved from the museums to the churches, to see the icons being used as they were meant to be. She was definitely right about one thing. In the thousand years of Russian icon painting, not one was ever painted to be hung in a museum. It was actually in a church that she met her friend Lyuda, whose brother ran the internet café. The first time Lyuda and Selia saw one another, they both spent a long time walking around the church looking at the icons, catching one another's eye. They had left the church at the same time, so that they had started talking. From Lyuda, Selia learned about variations in the different schools of icon painting, the Moscow school, the Novgorod school.

Sometimes Selia would tell Luke about elements of the paintings or about symbols in them, like the stars on Mary's forehead and shoulders. With such an interest, she began buying icons, but the more she knew, the more carefully she thought about what she was buying, wanting certain styles or subject matter. Slowly the walls of their apartment began to be hung with icons.

On one occasion Luke had reminded her how she used to see the icons. "You said they were flat and unrealistic," he said.

"They are flat and unrealistic," she answered. "They're supposed to be. I didn't know how to look at them. They're not supposed to be pictures of this world, with perspective and realism and shadows and correct colors. If that's what you expect, then you'll be disappointed when you look at them. But I learned that's not what they're about."

One of Selia's happiest moments was an occasion at a monastery when, by rare chance, she got into a conversation with a monk who turned out to be an icon painter, and for an hour the two of them sat on a stone wall near the gift shop and talked about how icons are painted and what they mean to the Orthodox religion. As Selia told Luke, an icon is not a picture of this world, and in some ways it might be considered not a picture at all, but a window. For the Orthodox faithful, as well as Luke understood it, an icon is a window into a spiritual world.

"OK," Paul said. "Maybe there's a letter stuck inside this desk somewhere. But yall know there's not."

"Yeah," Luke replied, "probably not." He was looking at Paul, who had kneeled down beside the desk and was holding the drawer.

"I'm using positive energy," Zoe said. "I think it's there."

Paul pulled out the middle drawer and set it on the floor, but he also looked in the drawer as he removed it, as if the letter would simply be lying there. Then he looked into the space where the drawer had been, saw nothing, and stuck his arm in. He concentrated on what he felt as he kneeled down, bending over, part of his arm inside the desk. He could feel ridges of wood and moved his fingertips along, concentrating for the flexible feel of paper.

"Any luck, then?" Carlee asked.

Paul's expression of concentration changed to surprise. "Yes," he said. "There's something stuck in there." A second later he pulled his arm out and was holding an envelope.

"Oh, my God!" Luke said. "I can't believe it."

"Why, you found it!" Carlee exclaimed. Zoe laughed to see the envelope.

Paul turned the envelope over, looking at both sides. "I don't know. There's nothing written on it." It looked like a plain white, modern envelope. He lifted the flap, which wasn't sealed, and pulled out two sheets of paper. They were yellowed and brittle, and he opened them carefully. "There's something here I can't read. It looks like it might be in Russian." He handed the sheets to Luke.

Luke took the pages carefully and studied the writing for a minute. "It's Russian," he said. He told them it was an older form of Russian, something written before the Revolution, but it wasn't what they expected.

"Would you prefer to sit down downstairs and look at it?" Carlee asked.

"Yes, let's do that."

Luke carefully folded up the letter and put it in the envelope again, and the four of them left the room, back out into the bright sunlight.

As Paul and Luke came in the door to the central cabin, Guy Hollingsworth turned around in his captain's seat, and his loud voice carried across the room. "Well any luck? Did you find the letter?"

"Yes!" Carlee exclaimed. "They found it!"

"We found something," Paul said. "We aren't sure what."

"You're not sure if it's a Russian letter?" Guy asked.

"It is a Russian letter," Luke said. "But I still need to look at it."

From this conversation other people in the room became interested. What Russian letter? Someone found a Russian letter? In Russian? How did that get on this boat?

"Can you read it?" asked Zoe. "This is kind of exciting."

Luke sat down on the leather couch. "It's not modern Russian," he said, "and the handwriting is a little difficult, but I think I can read it if I take my time."

A few people gathered around Luke where he sat, interested in the fact that something was going on.

Luke turned to his cousin. "The language in this is old, maybe what could have been used around Catherine the Great's time. I'm not an expert in that. But the letter isn't addressed to Middleton."

"Then who is it addressed to?"

"To a woman named Verochka."

"Oh, to a woman," Zoe said.

Paul felt stunned. "Verochka?" he said. "Verochka? Who is Verochka? Aunt Maryanne said the letter was to Henry Middleton."

"I don't know. Give me a minute to read it over. I just read the beginning there." Luke looked at the letter silently for a few minutes while the people around him grew restless. "OK," he said finally. "It's not from Catherine the Great. It's from a guy named

Ivan. It looks like he put his letter to Verochka in Henry Middleton's envelope."

"What? How do you—"

"I'll translate it," Luke said.

Дорогая Верочка, свѣтъ мой блестящий, какъ долго безъ тебя мнѣ жити? Лишь бы съ тобою я счастливъ, а безъ тебя нѣ могу терпѣть пустоту града. "Dear Verochka, my bright light," Luke began to translate. "How long will I be able to live without you? I'm only happy when I'm with you, and when you're not here, I cannot bear the emptiness of the city. You must come to Petersburg this fall." He was reading slowly and pausing. While he read, people were listening. "Princess Dashkova has asked me how you are enjoying life in the, uh…provinces, and asked that I bring you to see her when you are here again. You know that you have…have, um…enchanted me, my dear Verochka, simply cast a spell over me that I cannot escape. Every day I think about our walks in the Summer Garden, and I feel that I'm remembering the happiest moment of my life. Is it really possible that the, um…" Luke paused. "…that the cares of daily life could have stopped so completely, that I could have been so contented? I begin to think it was all an illusion. I will give you one bit of Petersburg gossip, but you must come here to get the rest. Everyone lately has gotten interested in, in uh…fortune telling, to find out what the future will be like. Count Shuisky has even brought an old serf woman in from one of his villages, a woman said to have the power to see what will happen to someone. The Count has held several soirées at his palace with the serf woman. I'm not sure I believe in fortune telling, but if it's true, the only future I want to hear predicted is that I will once again walk in the Summer Garden with you. I want to talk with you forever, but I must finish quickly. The Empress is leaving for the summer palace on the Gulf, and as part of the, uh…household staff, I must be ready in two hours. Even up until the last minute I am finishing up my duties here, with a letter to an American—" Luke stopped reading and looked quickly up at Paul. "—to thank him from the Empress for his views—"

"Henry Middleton!" Paul exclaimed.

"It doesn't say for sure," Luke said. "…with a letter to an American, to thank him from the Empress for his views, so I will mail your letter and his letter before I go. I am, and always will be, your captive, Ivan Alexeyevich."

Luke stopped reading and the room was silent for several seconds. "What a sweet letter," Zoe said.

"Why do we have this letter?" Paul asked, feeling very baffled.

Luke looked down at the papers in his hands, then said, "It looks like this guy put Verochka's letter in Henry's envelope. I guess she got Henry's letter."

Carlee said, "It's sad she never got the letter."

"I can't understand this," Paul said. "We finally track down the letter, and the original envelope is gone, and the letter isn't from Catherine the Great, and it isn't to Henry Middleton, but it is an old Russian letter. What the hell? Did anybody in our family ever read this?"

"Does your family read Russian?" Austin, the literature professor, asked.

"We think one of our ancestors did," Luke answered. He looked at Paul, then at Zoe, sighed, and shrugged his shoulders.

"This is really fascinating," Austin told Luke. "Maybe it appeals to the mystery scholar in me."

"Well, I guess it's a surprise letter," Guy said, his loud voice cutting through the rest of the conversation. "I guess that's it. If anybody wants to go fishing, I've got fishing gear in the room up front."

"I'd like to fish," said Paul. "But I'm going to go look in the desk again. I have to make sure there's not a second letter inside."

"I can tell you that from here," Luke said. "You might as well go fishing."

Zoe shook her head. "It really would be a kind of miracle, to find a second old letter in Russian."

"Yeah, I know," Paul said, and sighed. "I need a fishing pole."

The group standing around broke up, and some went to get fishing poles. Still not moving, Paul said to Luke. "If the second Henry Middleton was ambassador to Russia, he must have spoken Russian. Wouldn't he have read this letter? Why was it saved? Why was it even saved?"

"My God, who knows?" Luke said. "Who knows anything? Maybe it was just God's way of telling us to take a boat ride."

"I could have told you to take a boat ride," Zoe said. "If you asked."

"Yeah," Paul said. He looked out the large window at the water going by. "Yeah." A seagull swooped down low. "OK, I'm fishing. Did I mention that I love fishing?"

"Actually, I don't think you ever mentioned it," Luke said.

"I do. I really like to fish." Paul stopped and turned back to Luke. "I'm still going to write the book. I don't need the letter for that."

"And then you'll get tenure."

"Let God's lips speak those words."

"God doesn't have lips," Zoe said. "We're not even sure about ears."

An hour later Paul stood at the railing with a pole in his hand, feeling the breeze, watching the sparkle of light on the water. Farther down the railing, Luke and Zoe stood talking, but he couldn't hear their conversation. After a few minutes, Paul walked down that way.

"It's the best thing you could have found," Zoe said to Luke as Paul came up.

"Why is that?" Luke asked.

"How does it make you feel?" she asked. "It makes me feel sort of sad and sort of happy at the same time, thinking about those two people being in love. What could you have found that would have been better than that?"

"You could feel nothing but happiness."

"Don't ask for too much."

Luke looked at her a moment, then smiled a smile that might have also been sort of sad and sort of happy.

Paul started to say something about how useful the right letter would have been for his book, but then he forgot the book as a feeling washed over him of wishing Rachel was there, of wishing the four of them were standing at the railing watching the water.

When we read about real people like Paul and Luke, we are reminded that in the middle of the illusion we live in, there are actual people living their lives, people who eat dinner, who talk about the world, who fall in love. And perhaps it is not an illusion that they feel real hunger, real curiosity, real love. Above all, they feel real love, even if love comes and goes, even if people they love move in and out of their lives. When we are in love, we feel our hearts fly like a balloon, and when love is gone, we feel the ashes in our hands. That's no illusion.

Luke was sitting on Paul's balcony while Paul was gone to the store, and though it was still morning, already he could feel the heat of the day. Down the street people were talking, possibly tourists passing by, stepping out while the day was still a bit cooler. Luke looked at the view, not seeing it as his thoughts were still lost in the experience of finding the letter the day before. Such a strange odyssey they had been on, to finally arrive home and discover that they had never even left home. No letter from Catherine the Great. Luke wondered if Ivan had ever realized that Verochka didn't get his letter. She must have written back in some confusion. Did they meet again? Luke tried to picture them together with happy smiles when they saw each other, putting their arms around one another. He imagined them doing everyday things, as if it were him and Selia, having breakfast or pointing out someone interesting in the street. Did Ivan and Verochka marry? They were like the rest of humanity, their worries and hopes, the intensity of their passions, lingering kisses or tears of despair, all disappeared, as if they had never existed.

Luke heard voices and looked to see a couple walking past arm in arm. For a quick moment, he sensed the heavy feeling of missing Selia, but almost immediately he shoved the feeling away, to another part of his mind, in rebellion against misery. He didn't want to go the rest of his life drowning in sadness. That's not how anyone should live. He took a deep breath and looked at the pleasant scene in front of him. He knew that when he got home he would start going out again, trying to take pleasure from life, the way Selia did. She had known how to live, and he thought of how much she had liked Charleston the one time they had visited. He also liked Charleston, and he was definitely planning to come back soon.

Paul came out onto the balcony and sat down with Luke. "I got us some breakfast," he said. "A place down the street has the best bagels you ever ate."

"It's amazing," Luke said, "how many things you have the best of in Charleston."

"We're pretty damn lucky." Paul sat silently for a moment. He sighed, then said, "I'm a little scared, cousin. I've decided to go ahead and ask Rachel to move down here. I love her, and I want to be with her. But I'm scared."

Luke shook his head. "I've been thinking we can't live without fear, but if we aren't careful, we'll wind up living without everything else."

Paul looked over at his cousin. "Aren't you too young to be that wise?" he asked.

Luke sighed. "That's not wisdom. That's experience."

"Well, I'm going to call her today. I've got a house, and whatever happens with tenure, I want to be with her. I really want to."

"Good," Luke said. Neither spoke for a second, then Luke added, "I'm glad to hear you say that. But keep a room for me. I'd like to come back down for the Spoleto festival."

"Yeah, you should do that."

"Zoe said she'll go to the opera with me."

Paul looked at his cousin, raised one eyebrow, then smiled. "Let's go eat a bagel," he said.

"I'm looking forward to the best bagel I ever ate," Luke replied.

"It will be."

They stood and went into the apartment. Between the chairs where they had just been sitting, on the small table, Paul's African violet sat in the Gullah basket that Luke had bought the day before. A breeze blew by and from one side of the basket, the dried grass put out a live shoot, which rose and began to grow new green leaves.

* * *

David Hutto is a native of Georgia, currently living in Atlanta. He is a novelist and short-story writer, with an occasional hand in poetry, in addition to more quotidian forms of writing like academic articles on rhetoric or a newspaper health column. He has lived in fourteen states, with time in New York City and Washington, DC, and he has traveled six times to Russia, as a student, college professor, and tourist. His favorite type of wine is red.

His website is
www.davidhutto.com.